FELONIES AND FIREWORKS

WHISKEY MYSTERY #5

In Your Face Ink LLC
9524 W. Camelback Road
#130-182
Glendale, AZ 85305
www.inyourfaceink.com
www.whiskeydogmysteries.com

First printed in the United States of America by In Your Face Ink LLC

Copyright © 2025 by In Your Face Ink LLC

All rights reserved.

This is a work of fiction. Names, characters, places, and incidents either are the product of the author's imagination or are used fictitiously, and any resemblance to actual persons, living or dead, businesses, companies, events, or locales is entirely coincidental.

ISBN: 979-8-9924943-4-1 (hardback)
ISBN: 979-8-9924943-5-8 (paperback)
ISBN: 979-8-9924943-3-4 (e-book)

Book design and cover by Rick Schank of Purple Couch Creative

To all creatures great and small who aren't fans of fireworks,

we feel you.

RAP SHEET

CHAPTER 1

Red-haired Sarah Carter was grateful for a rare day off from Carter's Canine Coiffure, her dog grooming business in Cottageville, Iowa. So far, the year had been a whirlwind. February kicked off with the first annual Valentine's Day Pet Parade and related festivities, an idea Sarah and her assistant, Emily Holt, came up with after binge-watching too many dog videos on social media. During that same time, Sarah had helped the police solve two crimes: an arson case and the disappearance of an heirloom necklace and the high school football coach's prized autographed football.

March brought another kind of excitement, a less dangerous kind, when Sarah's parents flew in from Seattle for a couple week visit.

It was especially awesome since she hadn't seen them in almost a year.

From late March through April, Sarah supported her boyfriend, Jared Greene, as he took a break from his full-time job at Java and Juice so he could zig-zag around the country on a media tour promoting his graphic novel, which was released in April to critical acclaim. At the end of April, during a brief pause in his tour, Jared gave up his apartment above a garage and moved in with Sarah and her Australian red heeler cattle dog, Whiskey, into the Craftsman bungalow she had inherited from her grandmother, Gigi, about seven years earlier.

Since moving in, Jared had been juggling multiple responsibilities: his shifts at the cafe, owned by Sarah's best friend Ginger Jones, unpacking and unboxing his life, fulfilling his book promotion commitments, and working on his next graphic novel, which was due to his New York City publisher in the fall. Jared's rising popularity had kept him busy with podcast interviews, both morning and late show appearances, and some bookstore events on both coasts and in one of his favorite places, Chicago.

When Jared first moved to Cottageville after university, he chose the town for its affordable, art-filled community, where he could further his passions and eventually reach his goals of becoming an illustrator and author. Now, with some of his aspirations accomplished—including an invitation to give a keynote address at Comic-Con in San Diego—Sarah saw the toll that constant demands had taken on him and felt his exhaustion.

Today, while Jared worked at the cafe to make up for some of the hours he had been off, Sarah decided to surprise him by transforming her cluttered third bedroom into a suitable studio for Jared. She planned to install a reclaimed wood and wrought iron tiltable drafting table under the big backyard-facing windows, so Jared had plenty of natural light for his artwork. Her best friend's fiance Daniel Snyder, owner of Buck and Son hardware, was scheduled to deliver the table any minute.

But first, Sarah had to deal with Whiskey, who was outside in a staring death match with Mozart, the orange and white tabby belonging to Robert Wise, their neighbor from two doors up.

"Whiskey," Sarah yelled, "Mozart doesn't want to be herded. It's a cat thing. That's why he's hissing and arching his back. Leave the poor cat alone, boy."

Whiskey's rust-colored ears turned like they were satellites searching for signals. But he kept his eyes on the feline with its fur bristling along its spine like a wave frozen in time. Its narrowed eyes glinted with sharp intensity, a piercing gaze that seemed to warn against any approach. Ears flattened against its head, its tail lashed back and forth with a rhythm nothing like its namesake but that betrayed its tension.

And yet Whiskey wouldn't take the hint. He wanted Mozart to play with him and to *like* him. But time and again Mozart preferred to sit on their fence and taunt the dog rather than run, chase, or wrestle, like Whiskey did with his canine companions. Disdain oozed from the cat once he confirmed Whiskey couldn't reach him. He licked his arm leisurely while side-eying the dog.

Finally, Sarah had had enough. She marched into the side yard and grabbed her dog by his collar. "Come on, Whisk. We don't have all day."

That was a bit of a lie, since in truth, they did have all day. This Saturday in late June they had nothing on their schedule—except cleaning the house and setting up Jared's studio—until the evening. And at the moment, it was only ten a.m.

Just as Sarah coaxed Whiskey inside, he bolted to the front door, barking like marauders were storming the front yard. Sarah spied the Buck and Son delivery truck in her driveway so she opened the door wide. Whiskey took that as an invitation to greet his friend, Daniel, which he did with the exuberance of a sea otter with a sea urchin, licking his hand and closing his mouth around it and pulling like he was welcoming Daniel into their home.

Daniel laughed. "Give me a minute, bud, I have work to do."

Whiskey thumped his tail on the ground in anticipation.

Daniel's assistant stepped down from the passenger side of the truck. He was built like he wrestled professionally and maybe took steroids, and he introduced himself as Tiny Tim. Sarah's eyes widened in response to his name; she shook his proffered hand. Whiskey sat at Tim's feet and offered his own hand to the man, who leaned over and shook Whiskey's paw. "You have the coolest dog."

Sarah chuckled. "He certainly thinks so."

The men went around to the back of the truck, installed a metal ramp to the tailgate, and slid a dolly under the big crate. Tim tilted the crate toward himself on the dolly and walked it backwards down the ramp while Daniel spotted and called out directions and things to avoid. When they got to Sarah's small porch, Daniel placed a sturdy sheet of wood over her steps and he and Tim slowly guided the crate and dolly up the plywood and through her front door.

"Through the living room and down the short hallway and on the right," Sarah said, though she knew Daniel knew her house well since they were good friends.

Once they narrowly fit the crate through the bedroom door, Daniel asked Sarah where she wanted the desk. She pointed to the wall where the big windows were. "I figured it should be centered under the windows."

"Okay."

Tim removed a crowbar from his back pocket, and the crowbar bit into the narrow gap between the crate's lid and its sturdy frame, the metal scraping against wood with a grating screech. With a firm grip and a grunt of effort, Tim leveraged the tool downward, forcing the lid to creak and groan under the pressure. The wood resisted stubbornly at first, the nails holding fast like teeth clenched against intrusion. But with a sharp crack, the seal broke, and the lid splintered upward, revealing white foam sheeting protecting the metal and wood within.

With much noise that sent Whiskey running from the room, Tim removed the sides from the crate, and then he and Daniel lifted the table to the space Sarah had indicated. They let her cut cautiously through the foam with a box cutter until the beauty of the old reclaimed wood and the charcoal of the metal gleamed in a ray of light through the window.

"That's some table," Tim said.

"Sarah's boyfriend is Jared Greene, the artist,' Daniel explained.

"Ahh, that barista-turned-big-shot?" Tim nodded his head like he was impressed.

Sarah grinned at Daniel, feeling proud that people knew Jared's name.

"Need anything else?" Daniel asked Sarah.

"No. I'm good."

"Okay then. We'll get this packing and the crate parts out of your way and we'll be on our way. You may want to run a shop vac in here before Whiskey visits this room. There could be splinters."

"Good thinking," Sarah said. While the guys cleaned up the mess, she popped into her garage to get the cylindrical vacuum that had been in residence since her grandparents had lived in the house.

Sarah and Whiskey walked the men to their Buck and Son truck. Sarah shook Tiny Tim's massive hand once again and gave Daniel a hug and thanked them. And then she returned to the now-studio and shut Whiskey out of the room while she ran the shop vac. Then she set up the daylight lamp and stand so Jared would have plenty of light, installed his big wooden standing easel in a corner, also near the window, and moved the boxes he had stashed in the garage marked "STUDIO" into the space.

Sarah didn't want to overstep by opening any of the boxes so she left them for him to unpack and put away. At least the space now felt welcoming for work.

The rest of the time, until Jared came home at three, Sarah used to clean the two and a half bathrooms and the kitchen, to vacuum the rugs and mop the hardwoods, and to prepare a picnic for their supper. Tonight, they planned to attend the community movie at Cottageville Park.

Four hours later, Whiskey, off-leash as usual, Sarah, and Jared walked up their street and looked both ways before venturing over the cross-street and into the park. Sarah scanned the people in the park, as they planned to sit with three early-octogenarian friends: Gladys Rossmiller, who had been Gigi's best friend; Sarah's across the street neighbor Mrs. Janice Jenkins, who was now Gladys' closest friend; and Bill Reid, a widower whose company was sought after by Cottageville's gray-haired granny set and who seemed to be close to or dating both Gladys and Janice. Sarah carried a tote bag with bug spray; Whiskey's water and food; a big blue, black, and white Mexican blanket; and hers and Jared's sweatshirts in case it got chilly after the sun completely set. They were both currently in shorts and t-shirts. Jared carried the wicker picnic basket with their food, plates, and utensils, as well as a cans of wine and plastic stemware since glass wasn't permitted within the park.

Sarah spied Gladys in a pastel tracksuit and her two miniature poodles, Kahlo and Cassatt, with Bill a few yards away, so she walked in that direction, but of course, Whiskey beat her to the destination. He sniffed his friends and slurped Kahlo's ear with his big tongue. Bill, wearing jeans and a faded gray t-shirt, opened one lawn chair and then another and then a third, placing each in the grass facing the screen that looked wider and taller than Sarah's house.

"Take a seat, Glad." He motioned to the chairs and Gladys chose the one on the right. "Sarah, why don't you put your blanket in front of us and we'll put our cooler on your blanket, if you don't mind."

"That's fine by me," Sarah said. Once she and Jared had the blanket spread and all of their things laid out on top of it, she officially greeted Gladys and Bill with hugs and scratched under the poodles' chins.

Whiskey wandered nearby saying hello to Sascha the German shepherd and to Police Chief James Order and his wife Barbara and to some of his other friends.

Wearing pull-on linen pants and a lilac button-down shirt, Janice arrived with a tote filled with delicious delicacies and lowered herself into the left hand chair next to Bill, just as Mayor Trish McGowan spoke into the microphone. "Thank you, friends and neighbors, for coming for tonight's film. We offer the free Saturday night films and the Sunday evening concerts all summer long to foster a sense of community and to help you get to know one another. Tonight's film is the family-friendly *Inside Out*, a little over an hour and a half animated emotional rollercoaster that may have you laughing and crying in the same few seconds." Trish smiled. "And now on with the show."

Sarah asked Whiskey to return to their blanket and sit, which he did after lapping up some water. She placed his food bowl in front of him and he gobbled it down like he was in a world-record setting eating contest. "Slow down, Whisk," Sarah admonished. "Don't make yourself sick."

His brown eyes met her green ones like he had no idea what she was talking about. She shook her head and petted his neck. He laid down and cuddled against her leg.

Jared handed Sarah a plate of perfect picnic food: potato salad, baked beans, and chicken salad with celery and dried cranberries, of all of which Sarah made fresh earlier in the day. He also handed her a glass of Sauv Blanc, and quietly asked Bill, Gladys, and Janice if they would like anything. In unison, the three stopped chewing, gave Jared a smile, and politely responded, "No, thank you." They were enjoying smoked turkey and havarti sandwiches and a fruit salad Janice had made.

The movie started and Sarah was mesmerized by both the vibrant colors of the characters on screen as well as how relatable the story was. She had seen the movie before, when it first came out, but as it played before her, she realized how much of it she didn't remember… and why it had won an Academy Award. The storyline, the voice-over acting, and the animation were all so engaging and well-done.

Thirty or forty mesmerizing minutes into the film, Whiskey's eyes popped open and he wriggled his nose like he caught a scent. He released a whimper, which set Sarah on edge. "What is it?" she whispered to him. He popped up onto all fours and turned around staring at Bill, who suddenly grabbed his chest and opened his mouth, eyes bugging behind his glasses in fear.

Sarah's heart beat staccato in her chest. "Call nine-one-one," Sarah said aloud to Jared. "Bill's having a heart attack."

CHAPTER 2

arah grabbed ahold of Bill's hand and said, "Stay with me, Bill. Help is on the way."

Sweat beaded Bill's brow and he grimaced in pain.

"Has he had one before?" Jared asked, phone to his ear. "Does he take nitro?"

"No," Gladys said. "He's never had a heart attack. None of us have."

Janice Jenkins—who seemed to always be prepared in an emergency—rummaged in her bag for a few seconds and pulled out a single dose packet of aspirin, ripped it open, and held the pills in front of Bill's mouth, silently asking permission to pop them in. She grasped a bottle of water in her other hand.

Bill opened his mouth and accepted the pills like a baby bird taking a worm from its mother. He swallowed while Janice tilted the bottle of water into his mouth. His coloring was a pale gray like the underbelly of a fish.

"Five minutes out," Jared said, still on the line with emergency services.

"Will they be able to get through the crowd?" Gladys asked.

Chief James appeared behind Bill and put his hands on the man's shoulders. "Are you okay, Bill?"

Bill gasped a breath and his voice was shaky, but he was able to eke out an "Okay."

Sirens could be heard getting closer and then they suddenly stopped.

"Excuse me. Excuse me. Coming through," could be heard as Wendy and Walter Parks pushed the gurney over the bumpy park terrain and through the crowd of blankets and lawn chairs that were parting like the Red Sea for the biblical Moses.

When the Parks reached Bill, they checked his blood pressure, heart rate, and oxygen saturation levels, as well as his blood sugar level, before assisting him onto the gurney and strapping him down as well as hooking him up to a portable electrocardiograph. Chief James led the way out of the park, asking people to move again so they could get through, while Janice, Gladys, and her dogs trailed behind.

On the screen in front, the movie continued, its brightness and joviality a contrast to how Sarah now felt.

"What do you want to do?" Jared's hand was on Sarah's back

and his words were said next to her ear. "Want to take this stuff home and then go to the hospital?"

"I don't know." Sarah's eyes had narrowed and she frowned. "I don't want us to be in the way. Maybe we leave and see if Gladys wants us to keep her girls until she's done. She kept Whiskey for me while you were in the ER. I can return the favor."

Jared was already scraping the food from their plates back into the containers and then he snapped the lids closed. He restocked the picnic basket. He motioned toward her glass, signaling her to finish the wine in it. Two sips and it was empty.

Sarah folded the chairs left by her friends when they trailed after Bill and the Parks, while Jared was crouched on the ground to fold their blanket, while still allowing people to see over them to the big screen. Jared shoved the blanket into the tote bag and threw the tote over his shoulder before he picked up the picnic basket and stood. "Come on, Whiskey," he urged in a sharp whisper, as Sarah scooped up the chairs with a clatter and hurried behind them, walking as quickly as possible. She was determined to catch up with Gladys and her poodles.

In the park's parking lot, Wendy climbed into the ambulance after the stretcher and was pulling the double doors shut as Jared, Sarah, and Whiskey approached. Janice called into the closing doors, "We'll see you at the hospital, Bill."

Sarah said, "Wait. Gladys, why don't I take your dogs for the rest of the evening or even overnight. Whiskey and I can walk Kahlo and Cassatt home in the morning, if that's most convenient for you."

"That's so sweet of you, dear," Gladys said. "We have to go get Janice's car so I'll walk them that far." She eyed the navy blue camp chairs in Sarah's arms. "Thank you for getting the chairs. I forgot all about them. They belong to Bill."

"I can hang onto them until he's out of the hospital," Sarah said. "It's no problem."

Gladys nodded her head.

The four humans and their three canine companions walked—with Whiskey leading the way like a marshal in a parade—down the sidewalk on Janice's side of the street. At her mailbox, Jared reached for the poodles' leashes with his free hand. "Have they had dinner?" he asked.

"Yes, I fed them before we left for the movie," Gladys said.

"Anything special we need to know?" Sarah asked.

Gladys pursed her lips and narrowed her eyes as if she were thinking hard, and then said, "Cassatt sleeps with her head on a stuffed animal. Does Whiskey have one to spare and share?"

Sarah grinned. "He has plenty."

"But if we get out early enough, I may come pick them up, if that's okay. I'm not used to a quiet and empty house."

"Gladys, if you'd prefer us to walk them home right now, we can do that. Just loan us a key. Does Janice have a spare?"

"I do," Mrs. Jenkins said.

Gladys fished in her pocket and pulled out a key on a brass ring. "Please wait an hour or two, Sarah, before taking them home so they aren't by themselves for too long. I'll keep in touch on how things go."

"Okay," Sarah said. "And if you think you'll be at the hospital most of the night, we are happy to keep them." Sarah hugged Gladys and Mrs. Jenkins. "Give my love to Bill."

Then she and Jared, all of the picnic equipment, and the three dogs crossed the street to their home. As soon as the front door opened, Whiskey trotted to his water bowl and Sarah could hear his loud slurps and his metal tags ding off the bowl. Cassatt and Kahlo strained at their leashes like they wanted to join him so Sarah set the folded chairs against the wall next to her front door and then bent and quickly unclipped them, setting them free to scamper into the kitchen.

Jared trailed after them with the picnic basket. "I didn't have time to eat much so I'm going to prepare a plate. Do you want one, too?" He pulled a dinner plate from the cupboard and when Sarah nodded her head he grabbed one for her also. He set them on the counter and then pulled the contents from the basket.

Sarah retrieved two wine glasses and uncorked a bottle of wine they had opened last night. "Do you think Bill will be okay?" she asked as she poured a few ounces into each glass.

"I'm sure he will, but I'm guessing we'll know for sure in a few hours."

"I've never been near someone while they were having a heart attack."

"Me neither." Jared carried the two plates of food and forks into the dining room.

"But Whiskey seemed to sense what was going on even before it happened."

At the sound of his name Whiskey released a single bark, which caused Sarah and Jared to chuckle. "Research says dogs can smell cancer and can sense when someone's blood sugar levels are too high. Must be changes they can sniff or feel before a heart attack, too." Jared sat at the table and dug into the potato salad. After he swallowed he said, "You really outdid yourself with the food. It's all so good."

Sarah grinned. "Thank you. I learned from one of the best." She reached across the table and squeezed his hand. Sarah had mastered basic cooking skills in childhood, but since Jared had moved in, she observed and learned from him, elevating what she could do in the kitchen...and what was most surprising to her was that she found she enjoyed the creativity of combining ingredients into new taste sensations. But she was still lightyears away from Michelin star worthiness.

After they finished the food, Sarah cleaned the dishes and put away the leftovers while Jared accompanied the fur children into the fenced backyard. He brought two different size balls with him, Whiskey's usual tennis ball and a smaller rubber ball more suited to the mouth size of the miniature poodles. Jared threw Whiskey's ball first and the cattle dog raced after it like he was determined to get gold in the Olympics. Kahlo stood next to Jared watching Whiskey go. Cassatt followed her nose on an invisible trail to the fence that ran along the right side of the house.

"What do you smell?" Jared asked. "Mozart? A raccoon? A squirrel?"

Casssatt ignored his questions.

"Ready, Kahlo?"

At her name, Kahlo's ears perked.

"Get ready, Kahlo." Jared said, moving his arm backwards before launching it and the ball into the air. "Go get it."

Without further encouragement, Kahlo launched herself to the end of the yard, scooping the small red ball from the grass, doing a one-eighty, and running back to Jared, where she dropped the ball next to his bare foot.

"Good girl," Jared enthused, scratching the top of Kahlo's curly head.

Back and forth the dogs ran and fetched and returned and eventually Cassatt abandoned the trail of smells for the boisterous ball activity. When all three dogs lay on the grass, tongues protruding from their open mouths, panting, Jared declared it was time to go inside.

"They are going to sleep well tonight," he told Sarah.

All three dogs simultaneously slurped water from Whiskey's bowl before crashing on the kitchen floor.

"Any word yet?" Jared asked, getting himself a glass of tap water.

"Gladys texted that they have just been taken back to see Bill. Apparently the three of them have each other listed as medical POA."

"Really? I didn't know you could have more than one power of attorney."

"I didn't either. But I looked it up and it's a thing." Sarah glanced down at her phone on the counter.

"Gladys said they will keep him overnight for observation, but that he's doing okay. She and Janice will stay another hour or until they move him to a room. We can take the dogs back whenever we are ready." Sarah's eyes trailed to the three furry lumps stretched on their sides on the floor.

"Should we let them rest first or do you want to go now?"

Sarah eyed the time. "If we go now we may miss the crowd in the park."

Jared raised one red eyebrow. "Or we could run smack into them."

"We'll take the streets instead of cutting through the park. Or we'll cut through the part further down, closer to Main Street." Bill's house was on Main Street north of the park's entrance and Gladys was three doors up from him. On Sarah and Whiskey's daily morning walk, they traveled up their street, through the park, stopping by Bill's for a biscuit, and often a chat, and then back through the park and home.

"Okay," Jared said. "Give me a few minutes first," as he headed into the nearest bathroom.

Sarah squatted in between the poodles and patted their heads. "You girls ready to go home? Gladys will be there shortly. I'm sure she misses you."

Kahlo rolled one eyeball up at Sarah, but Cassatt kept her eyes closed and let out a sigh. Sarah smiled down at them, remembering how she was with Gladys when she picked them out of close to a dozen dogs at Daisy and Donovan's poodle rescue. They had gone for one dog after Gladys had said goodbye to Oodle and returned with two affectionate girls who added color and activity to Gladys' world that had dimmed after the death of her companion of at least a decade and a half.

"I'm ready," Jared announced, coming into the kitchen. He had thrown a blue and black flannel shirt over his t-shirt and donned running shoes and socks. Whiskey stood and stretched and then walked to the front door like he understood exactly what was going on. He looked back over his shoulder and released a sharp "yip" that called the poodles to attention and their nails clicked on the hardwood floors as they sped to join him.

Sarah picked up their harnesses and put them on and then attached their leashes.

"Should we take the chairs and put them on Bill's porch?" Jared asked.

"Nah. Let's wait until he's home. We'll return them then and bring him some soup or something."

"Okay. Good plan. Do you have Gladys' key? I have ours."

Sarah grabbed Gladys' house key from a bowl on the console table near the front door. "I do now. Thanks for the reminder." She leaned up and kissed Jared's scruffy cheek.

As they walked up the hill, they could hear laughter and voices coming from the park. The movie seemed to have ended, but people loitered, enjoying the fine summer evening.

Whiskey snapped his jaws at a lightning bug that had the audacity to illuminate to the right of his head.

"Don't eat too many of those, Whisk," Sarah said.

He cocked his head over his shoulder and eyed her. "I'm serious. I know you're defending your space, but fireflies can make your tummy sick."

"And we really don't want to deal with glowing poop tonight," Jared added with a smirk.

"Eww, gross," Sarah remarked as Jared grabbed her free left hand and entwined his fingers with hers, swinging their hands and arms between their bodies as they walked. Whiskey walked a half-body length in front of Jared, next to the poodles, when they weren't stopping to sniff or to pee on something.

In the descending darkness, they walked up Main Street, where red, white, and blue bows adorned every streetlight, and passed Bill's house where Sarah said a silent prayer that Bill be okay and come home quickly. The house next to Bill's was in complete darkness, like its occupants weren't there. And the house after that had been converted into an antique shop. Its front bay windows were topped with red, white, and blue bunting for the upcoming holiday and were lit year round by old-fashioned electric taper candles. Through the glass Sarah could see the clutter of furniture, an old wooden carousel horse, lamps, vases, and glass-fronted bookshelves crammed with tomes.

But as they passed the store and climbed the stairs for Gladys' front porch, something registered in Sarah's subconscious. A window on the south side of the antique store looked jagged and broken. Sarah's eyes narrowed as she went inward reviewing the image in her head... and she missed inserting the key into Gladys' lock.

"You okay?" Jared asked.

She shook her head, causing her ponytail to bounce. "I think there's a broken window at the antique store."

"I didn't notice. But we can check it out once the girls are safely inside. Have you gotten any more texts from Gladys?"

Sarah inserted the key into the lock properly this time and pushed the door open. Whiskey ran into the house as if he was the welcoming committee. The poodles strained after him so Sarah set them free and then chased after them to remove their harnesses.

Jared turned on the lights in Gladys' kitchen and refilled the poodles' water bowl. He gave all three dogs treats from a jar on the counter after making them sit on command. Sarah watched him give Gladys' kitchen door that led into her backyard a thorough look before he walked toward it.

He turned the handle and opened the door and looked out into the backyard. "This wasn't locked, Sarah."

Sarah shrugged. "Maybe she forgot."

"Maybe." Jared said, shutting and locking it. "But just in case, I'm going to do a walk-thru."

"The dogs would have alerted us if someone was in the house. I'm sure it was just an oversight." Sarah stayed in the kitchen with the poodles while Jared and Whiskey wandered from room to room. She pulled her phone from her shorts' pocket and checked for any new texts.

When Jared returned to the kitchen, Sarah said, "Gladys said they are leaving in ten minutes. Bill has been moved to a room, and the doc said he'll most likely be released in the morning so they will go back and pick him up then."

"That's good news." Jared hugged her. "Do you want to wait for them here?"

"No. I want to see if my eyes were playing tricks or if the window really is broken at the antique store."

"Okay. Then let's lock up and be on our way."

As they walked through the living room they found Kahlo and Cassatt curled together on the sofa. Sarah patted their heads. "Your mom will be home soon, girls. We love you. Have a good nap." She locked the door and followed Jared and Whiskey down the stairs.

"Which side of the building?" Jared asked as he walked down

the sidewalk with his head turned, eyes searching the store.

"The side toward Bill's."

Jared stopped on the sidewalk in front of the big windows and strained his neck toward the building. "You're right. From here it looks broken. Let's cut down the side and check it out." He led the way past the front of the store and around the azaleas that flanked the side of the two-story former home. About fifteen feet from the sidewalk, the window that was four feet from ground level sported a jagged, gaping hole. A few black threads were caught on the sharpest piece of glass.

Jared turned on his phone's flashlight and shined the beam into the store's darkness while Sarah called the police.

CHAPTER 3

Five minutes later a patrol car pulled up the curb, and Officer John Beams greeted Whiskey first and then Jared and Sarah. His black curls cradled his cap and his muscles stretched his uniform. Sarah, Jared, and Whiskey led him to the broken window.

John's flashlight illuminated the ground around them, but nothing looked disturbed. "The Chief is calling the Maslows. They are out of town for their daughter's graduation from med school."

Sarah had grown up in Seattle, and even after more than seven years in Cottageville, she sometimes forgot how the community members knew so much about each other's day-to-day lives. "Were they closed for the weekend?"

"Nah. Micas Brighton was filling in. We'll see what time he closed. You didn't try to go in, did you?"

Sarah shook her head no as Jared said, "No, we didn't."

Sarah had met Micas Brighton only once at a community picnic. She could picture his shock of white mad scientist hair and his piercing blue eyes highlighted by wrinkles from years of squinting. He was a retired historian who wasn't super social and lived on the outskirts of town.

John led the trio to the front of the antique store, where he donned gloves before trying the front door. Much to Sarah's surprise, it opened. "Why would anyone break the window to get in if the door was unlocked?" she asked.

"It probably wasn't. But going through the front door with a larger item is way more convenient than back out the window," John said. "Stay here." He drew his sidearm and held it in front of himself along with the flashlight before yelling, "Police," and stepping into the store.

Sarah watched his back for a second and then said to Jared, "Let's stand off to the side. If he gets shot at or someone comes running, I don't want to be in the line of fire or the way." She had a hold of Whiskey's collar, otherwise the dog would have accompanied the cop into the store.

"You've been watching too many police shows again." Jared smiled at her. "This isn't NYC. Cottageville PD rarely fire their weapons, except at the gun range. They've had no need."

Sarah thought back to when Mrs. Jenkins had disappeared and realized that what Jared said was true. When the bullets started flying, it was the feds involved in the gunfight. She made a mental note to ask Candace Grimes, one of her close friends and the only female on the CPD force if she had ever had to draw her weapon or shoot anyone.

Sarah lost sight of John or even his light as he made his way through the back rooms of the antique store. As soon as she saw the arc of light again, it was ascending the stairs that were midway through the building, Jared touched her arm and said, "There are Janice and Gladys."

Sarah turned back toward the street as Janice's car pulled into Gladys' driveway. Whiskey let loose a whine when the two women exited the car. He strained against the hold Sarah had on his collar. "Hey, I'm gonna ask her about the back door," Sarah said. "Now that we know this place was broken into, I'm rethinking my initial idea."

"That's probably wise. I'll wait here for John."

Sarah followed Whiskey up the sidewalk to Gladys and Janice, who asked, "What's going on?"

Gladys worked her knobby arthritic fingers in Whiskey's thick copper and white fur.

"Break-in. We noticed a busted side window and called the police. John Beams is inside checking it out. Hey Gladys, when we took the girls home, we noticed your kitchen door wasn't locked. Did you...um...maybe forget?"

Gladys frowned. "No. I'm sure it was locked. I used the key, as the girls and I left our house through the backyard to the park."

"Give me your key, Glad," Mrs. Jenkins said, her training of working for government alphabet agencies clearly kicking in.

"Jared and Whiskey did a complete walk-through when we

noticed the door unlocked. Oh and here." Sarah pulled the key from her pocket and handed it to Gladys.

"Thank you, dear," Gladys said as she handed the other key— the spare—back to Janice.

"Did anything look disturbed?" Mrs. Jenkins asked.

"I don't think so," Sarah said, before calling out to Jared, "Hey, Jare, everything looked okay next door, right?"

"Yes. A bedroom window was open an inch, but I figured that was normal this time of year around here."

"Yes, those I left open," Gladys said.

"Thank you for letting us know, Sarah," Janice said. "I'll walk through with Gladys to make sure no valuables are missing."

"How's Bill?"

"He'll be fine," Gladys said as she and Janice climbed her front stairs. "The doctor said we did all of the things we should have and got him there quick enough."

"That's great news. Have a good night. I'm sure your girls are thrilled you're home. Come on, Whiskey," Sarah said, since her dog was climbing the steps after the women.

Officer Beams exited through the open front door of the antique store and Whiskey ran to meet him. "It's empty," John said, "and I can't really tell if anything was taken. There are a few drops of blood on the floor here and there, like the person cut themselves breaking in or coming through the window. The lab guys will be here shortly. Thanks for calling this in, Sarah."

"Of course. And just so you know, Gladys' back door was unlocked when we got to her house, and she swears she locked it with the key before heading to the park. Maybe we should check Bill's doors and the other neighbor's too. Do you think someone figured most of the town would be at the movie so it was a good night to hit a bunch of houses?" A chill shivered through Sarah at the thought as the words left her mouth.

"Was anything taken from Gladys?" John asked, eying her house.

"Not that we could tell, but she and Janice are going through it now."

"When the lab gets here, I'll go over and see them and then I'll check Bill's doors, as I heard about his heart attack."

"We can check as we go past," Sarah offered.

"No, Sarah. I'll do it. I have the gloves and am the law." John smirked at her and his hazel eyes sparkled in the porch light.

Jared reached for Sarah's hand. "We should get home. I promised G I'd go in early and help with the donuts the Presbyterian church ordered for tomorrow's before-service social."

"Ooo, I forgot all about that. Come on, Whiskey. It's time for bed," Sarah said. "Good night, John."

The park had mostly emptied of movie goers. A few teens, clustered into couples, were on the swings and perched atop the jungle gym. The moon shone brightly overhead making it easy to see the path that bisected the green space from Main Street to Park Street. Whiskey followed his nose, meandering to the left and then back toward the right before bolting after something in a shrub ten feet away.

"Leave it," Sarah commanded as he rooted at the base of the foliage.

"Leave it," Sarah said a second time. "Let it be, Whiskey."

He pulled out his head and then shook the small leaves from his fur and trotted back to her, his black mouth pulled back into a smile as if he was super proud of himself.

Sarah ruffled his ears. "Good boy."

On the way down the sidewalk to their house, Jared said, "I've been thinking about what you said back there. You know, about someone targeting homes and the business because everyone was at the park. You may be on to something. If I was going to rob places, I'd want to ensure that they were empty. There's not much better time than when everyone—police chief included—are preoccupied with something together."

"I wonder if anyone's house was robbed during the last movie in the park or during any of the Sunday concerts." Sarah pulled out her phone and texted Officer Beams asking that question.

"With how small our town is and the way everyone talks, we'd know if someone was robbed during the community events."

"I guess," Sarah said.

"Java and Juice is gossip central."

"That's because Barbara and Trish are there every morning," Sarah said. Mrs. Chief and her BFF, the mayor, frequented the cafe most mornings before or after Barbara went to yoga class. She and Trish could be found at a table by the door, chatting with the townspeople, listening to complaints, and encouraging Cottageville spirit, as they had lived in the town for their whole lives. Cottageville's retired long-term mayor, Trish's father, liked to joke that Java and Juice was his daughter's second office.

Jared inserted his key into the door when Sarah's phone chimed with an incoming text. Sarah pulled the phone from her pocket while Whiskey burst into their house. "John says no burglaries during last week's movie or concert. Both Bill's front and back doors were unlocked, but Janice says he never locks them."

"Wow. Never?" Jared put his keys on the console table and locked the door behind them. "You want the alarm set tonight?" When Sarah's life had been threatened earlier in the year, Bill had overseen the installation of a security system and cameras. But since Jared had moved in, Sarah rarely set the alarm.

"Nah. We'll be fine." Whiskey beat them to the bedroom where he jumped on the bed and walked in a circle at the foot, causing the comforter to fluff and bunch, just how he wanted it, before curling into a ball atop it. "

"Uhh, you took most of the covers, dog." Sarah said, trying to ease the comforter from under him.

Whiskey let loose a loud, disgusted sigh.

"Here," Jared said, handing Sarah an afghan her grandmother had made her. Sarah kept an heirloom quilt and four Gigi-crocheted blankets in a cedar chest at the foot of her bed. "Though it is warm enough tonight we may be okay with just the sheets."

"That's true." Sarah opened the window closest to her side of the bed. She liked fresh air during the night and to hear the crickets.

"Goodnight, babe," Jared said, leaning over to kiss her before he slid between the sheets.

Sarah knew the five hours he had to sleep would not be enough. By the time she washed her face, got undressed and into a cartoon dog tank and shorts sleep set, and big-spooned Jared in bed, both Whiskey and Jared were already snoring in concert. She snuggled against her man and willed her mind to stop whirling about the break-in.

But eight hours later, while Jared was finishing the donuts at Java and Juice, Sarah's mind went into overdrive when she opened her front door and picked up her copy of *The Cottageville Courier*. In a large font above the fold the headline blared: "Rash of Burglaries Rock Residents". In a quick scan of the lede and first paragraph, Sarah learned that five houses or businesses had reported break-ins after the community movie. The article didn't specify what was stolen or how much anything was worth, but did quote one man as saying his "valuable coin collection and a stack of cash had been taken," which made Sarah question who kept stacks of cash? She certainly didn't. Nor did the people she was close to.

She perused the rest of the paper while she drained her first cup of coffee, and then she took a quick shower, dressed, and took Whiskey for his first walk of the day. Up the street, a loop through the empty park, and back down again. Whiskey seemed to understand that Bill was not home to give him a treat and that Java and Juice was closed since it was Sunday.

At seven-thirty, when Sarah thought it was late enough not to wake Gladys, she texted her elderly friend. "Was everything okay at your house? The Courier wrote about a number of burglaries yesterday."

Halfway through Sarah's second cup of coffee, the three texting dots appeared, followed by words. "Good morning. Everything is fine. Nothing is missing."

Weird, Sarah thought. *If Gladys really had locked her back door, how did it get unlocked? Maybe she put the key in to lock it and turned it the wrong way.* Sarah had done that once or twice herself.

"Thank you again for caring for my girls," Gladys texted.

"Any time," Sarah wrote. She stretched and put a couple of slices of sourdough bread into her toaster oven. While it browned, she sliced some avocado and swiss cheese.

Her doorbell chimed, interrupted the silence, and sent Whiskey into a barking and racing to the door frenzy. When Sarah caught up with him, she found Candace Grimes, in uniform, standing on her porch.

CHAPTER 4

"**H**ey. What brings you to my house at this hour? Did you smell the coffee and toast?"

"I wish it were a social call," Candace said. "Maple would love a play date." Maple was Candace's companion, an adopted mini lop rabbit the color of syrup. At first the rabbit was wary of the curious cattle dog, but after some supervised meet-and-greets, the two had become good friends.

"You and Maple are always welcome," Sarah said. "Want a cup of coffee? Some sourdough avocado toast while we conduct business?"

"I'd love some," Candace said. "I need your official statement from last night."

"I don't have much to say. I saw the busted window as we walked past and did my civic duty and phoned it in." Sarah poured a dark roast java into a cattle dog mug and passed it to Candace, whom she knew, like her, took her coffee black. The oven chimed signaling the end of the toasting and Sarah put one slice on each plate and smashed the avocado onto it. "Do you want cheese too?"

"On the side. Thank you."

Sarah passed Candace a plate and put two more slices of bread into the oven to toast.

"So, humor me and walk me through last night including the timeline."

Sarah took a bite of toast and swallowed and then went through the movie at the park, Bill's heart attack, the dogs, and then walking them home around eight, maybe eight fifteen.

"How did you notice a window broken on the side of the antique store?" Candace asked, scribbling Sarah's answers and chewing her toast.

"You could see it through the front windows. It was jagged." Sarah frowned. "Maybe the moonlight hit it just right or something. At first I thought my eyes played a trick. So after we got Kahlo and Cassatt settled, Jared and I stopped at the store to check. And that's when we saw the screen bent and in the bushes and the smashed window and I called you."

"But you didn't go into the store or check any other windows or the doors?"

"No. We waited on the sidewalk in front until John showed up. And then we followed him down the side of the building again and then onto the front porch and waited there while he went inside to do a search."

"You didn't see anyone lurking around Main Street or notice anyone who looked out of place?"

"We saw no one until Gladys and Janice arrived at Gladys' in Janice's car. Then Whiskey and I went to talk to them about Gladys' door being unlocked when we arrived at her house."

Candace nodded her head. "That was in John's report."

"What kinds of things were stolen? The paper said a coin collection and some cash. But what else?" Sarah asked, slathering the two fresh-from-the-oven slices of sourdough toast with avocado and passing one to Candace.

"At the antique store we still aren't sure. We may have to wait for the Maslows to get home and tell us. But from the homes, some jewelry, one gun someone hadn't locked up..." Candace's eyes narrowed in disgust at that..."and a long leather coat and three pairs of heels from Daphne Smith's."

Sarah eyebrows shot up almost to her hairline. "Daphne's was one of the houses robbed?" Daphne Smith was famous—or infamous—in their town for being a Cottageville native and speaking mostly French though she had never been to France nor Quebec or Montreal or anywhere French was the official language. Her sweet French bulldog Pierre was one of Sarah's favorite clients since he was cooperative, docile, and preferred to be clean. Daphne was always impeccably dressed and tended towards classic fashion with clean lines, high heels, and often hats.

"Why would someone steal shoes?" And just as Sarah asked,

answers flooded her brain: fetish, to give to a loved one if the size was right, to resell if designer.

"They were designer," Candace said, "so maybe to sell for cash. Red soles and all of that." She waved her hand like swatting a gnat.

"Ah. I'm so sorry to hear that she was robbed. I can't imagine having someone come into my personal space like that."

"That echoes what she said last night. John reported she used words like violated, and that her sanctuary was no longer sacred...at least that's what he thought she said. His high school French is super rusty."

"Is it okay if I reach out to her? Were she and Pierre at the park? I didn't see them, but then again, it was crowded, and we weren't there for long."

"Yes, they were. She said toward the far left and way in the back. I think it is fine to contact her. None of the places were trashed or anything so there was nothing for people to clean up. It seems the robbers either went through windows or unlocked doors." Candace shrugged. "You know how this town is. I bet three out of four houses don't lock their doors ever or only at night or if they go on vacation."

"Even since that one Main Street bar started attracting bikers and such?"

"Yep. It's a mix of Mr. Rogers mentality and the mindset of 'I've got nothing of value to steal.'" Candace finished her last swig of coffee and then rose to walk her mug and plate to the sink. "Thanks for the breakfast. If you think of anything, text me."

"I will. I'm still trying to understand how five places get robbed in the span of a couple of hours. It's ballsy. But also sounds orchestrated.

Do you think it was more than one person? Like maybe a small gang that hit all of the places together or split up?" Sarah and Whiskey walked Candace toward the door.

"We aren't sure. We're low on clues."

"There were black threads stuck to a shard on the antique shop's broken window."

Candace turned toward Sarah and smiled. "Leave it to you to notice something like that, Sarahlock Holmes."

Sarah cracked up at the nickname. "Very funny. Thanks for stopping by." She hugged her friend and then shut the door as Candace walked to her patrol car.

Sarah checked the time on her smart watch. Jared should be home soon, but first she wanted to make a phone call.

Daphne answered after two rings. *"Allo?"*

"Bonjour, Daphne. It's Sarah. I wanted to check in. How are you? I heard you were robbed yesterday."

"Oui. C'est dérangeant."

Sarah wasn't sure if *dérangeant* meant deranged or disturbing but to whichever, she agreed. "It's absolutely terrible," she said. "Do you need anything? Earlier in the year when I was being sent those threats, I had a security system installed. Would you like the name and contact information for that company? Do you plan on adding cameras or an alarm system?"

"Oui. Je voudrais ces informations. Merci."

"Hang on one second and I'll send it to you." Sarah took a photo of the business card and texted it to Daphne.

"Merci," Daphne said again.

"Do you need anything else? I'm so sorry this happened to you."

"Merci, Sarah. Non. Ça va. Merci d'avoir appelé. Au revoir." With that she disconnected and Sarah was left listening to the dial tone, wondering if Daphne was really as okay as she said.

Jared walked through the front door a few moments later, much to Whiskey's joy. He raced to greet him and smiled showing his gums and teeth. "Give me five, my man," Jared demanded.

Whiskey sat on his furry butt and threw his right paw into the air hitting Jared's hand.

"And for you, mi'lady," Jared pulled a fuschia pink tea rose from behind his back and kissed her cheek. "Robert Wise was deadheading his bushes and told me to give it to you."

"How nice of him." Sarah breathed in the sweet scent of Grandma's Blessing, a varietal that grew well in their area. She carried the rose into the kitchen and pulled a skinny vase from the cupboard above the refrigerator where she kept things she used infrequently.

Jared asked, "What have you been up to?"

"Oh this and that. Did you know five places were broken into last night?"

"I heard people talking about thefts when we delivered the donuts to the church, but I hadn't heard the number." Jared poured himself a glass of water from the tap and drank it down.

"Do you think a burglary ring was working in Cottageville last night?" Sarah's eyes were sharp with curiosity.

Jared leaned against the counter, setting the empty glass down with a quiet clink. "I mean...five in one night doesn't feel random."

Sarah nodded slowly.

"At the church, Mrs. Dunkin said someone tried her back door around midnight but her dog scared them off. But she lives way out on Orchard Lane."

"I wonder if the gossip network had alerted her to the other thefts. Some of the old timers here listen to the police scanner. They may have heard the calls and dispatch. Maybe she was on high alert."

"Maybe," Jared said.

"I mean, I'm not calling her a liar, but I wonder. From what I can tell, the others were sort of clustered, or at least all were in town. The newspaper wasn't specific on locations, but Candace was here to take my statement. She said Daphne Smith's house was hit. That's right in town. The antique shop, too." Sarah pulled picnic leftovers from the refrigerator. "Are you hungry?"

"Yes. Three donuts don't last long."

Puffing up her cheeks and swaying back and forth like a weeble-wobble, "Wow. That's a lot of sugar and fat." Sarah giggled at her bean pole of a boyfriend.

"The energy of a hummingbird," Jared joked.

"Let's get something more substantial and healthy into you. Humans can't live on simple carbs alone."

"No, they need caffeine, too." Jared grinned at her and then leaned forward for a kiss. "So what else did Candace say?"

"Not much. You know, ongoing investigation and all that. Lips mostly closed."

"I prefer when yours are open." Jared stole another kiss, and then said, "Hey, Ginger wanted to know if we wanted to meet her and Daniel for the concert this afternoon. Did you want to go?"

"Umm." Sarah wondered if the burglar or burglars would strike two days in a row. "We could. I'd love to see them, though with the music and all, we can't be too social." Sarah loaded two plates with the leftovers and carried them to the dining room.

Jared trailed after her with utensils and napkins and a dehydrated pig's ear for Whiskey, who followed after him like he was HRH of Dog Treats. "So should I text G yes?"

"I guess. Is that the way you want to spend a couple of hours this afternoon?"

"As long as I'm with you, it's all good." Jared flashed her a lopsided smile.

"Oh brother." Sarah smirked and rolled her eyes goodnaturedly.

"And with Whiskey, too, of course," Jared added, but the dog was busy with his mouth gnawing on the ear he held between his two front paws. The best part of the dehydrated pig ears—besides helping create little animal waste in a snout to tail consumption kind of way—was that the eating of said ear took a long time. Too many other treats were gone in a snap of the jaw, causing Whiskey to beg for more.

Between bites of chicken salad, Jared said, "I'm going to unpack some boxes in the studio after we eat and maybe try to sneak in a nap."

"Sounds good. I'll review my schedule for the week, call my parents, and maybe even poke around the internet to see if any towns around us had a rash of burglaries in one night."

"You think this wasn't local?"

"No idea. But my investigation has to start somewhere." Sarah's smile was bright and wide and lasted until Jared said, "Umm, you have a bit of baked bean stuck between your top front teeth."

Sarah's hand flew over her mouth, and she worked her index fingernail between those two teeth. When she flashed her teeth again at Jared, she asked, "Did I get it?"

"Yep. All clean."

"Well, I'll get to it then." Sarah stood and carried her plate back into the kitchen and put it and her fork in the dishwasher.

CHAPTER 5

Four hours later, Jared, Sarah, and Whiskey stood outside their front door, locking it and setting the alarm. Sarah was still stuck in limbo's waiting room on whether it was necessary, but Jared reminded her that he was a bit more of a public figure than he used to be so it was better for them to be cautious than regretful. And with that reasoning she couldn't argue.

Jared was carrying the picnic basket again, but this time it contained a charcuterie board he had put together with meats and cheeses, olives, cornichons, grain-free crackers, and small screw top containers of mustards and pepper jellies. He had also packed the extra cans of wine they had in the fridge plus some bottles of water. Ginger had promised to bring fresh fruit and individual sized *pot de creme*. Sarah carried Whiskey's bowls and food and a few pet waste bags just in case. She also pocketed his leash, though they rarely used it. The red heeler cattle dog led their parade of three up the hill, though just as they were passing his home, Robert Wise popped out his front door with a soft-sided cooler. He grabbed a lawn chair off his front porch and joined them on their journey.

"I love these Sunday afternoon summer concerts," Robert exclaimed. "Two of my students are performing today." He wore a maderas shirt with the sleeves rolled to just below his elbows and chino shorts like he had stepped from a Ralph Lauren ad.

"That's wonderful," Sarah said. "And thank you, Robert, for the rose. That was so sweet of you to share."

"Any time, Sarah. Any time. I wish Mozart would walk on a leash or sit nicely in one of those strollers, but he's too fond of his freedom. And it's a shame because then he misses out on these concerts."

Jared grinned at him. "I'd think the crowd would be too much for him."

"True. True. I just get jealous how Whiskey wants to go everywhere."

At hearing his name, Whiskey turned around and took a few steps towards Robert. When they were in touching distance, Whiskey rubbed against his leg acting more cat than dog.

The three humans cracked up.

"I swear he understands everything we say," Robert said.

"He sure seems to," Sarah said.

No cars were traveling on Park Street so they crossed over into the lot and then into the grass.

"I'm gonna sit right in front where my students can see me," Robert said. "I'll catch you later. It's gonna be so fine." And he veered toward the center of the stage.

Sarah watched the families sprawled on blankets, valiantly attempting to keep their kids from escaping like tiny, corn syrup fueled fugitives. Some of the moms were laying out spreads that looked like mostly junk food: chips, plastic bottles of soda, Cheetos, and the like… or at least that's what they had pulled out of totes so far. The thought zipped through her mind: *Is this what Jared and I will be like when we have kids?* Yikes. Just watching them felt like a full-body workout. She didn't see Daniel or Ginger anywhere so she checked her phone.

No messages.

"Did they say where they wanted to sit?" Sarah asked Jared.

Whiskey wandered close to a man Sarah didn't know. He was putting a cracker topped with an orange cheese into his mouth. Whiskey's nose wiggled and he leaned toward the man like he wanted to snatch the snack from his hand. "Whiskey. No," Sarah said. "Heel."

He rolled his eyes up at her and then instantly reported to her side.

"You can't help anyone eat their food. You have your own." She patted his head and he looked up at her with love in his expressive brown eyes.

"There they are." Jared pointed toward the parking lot as Ginger exited the passenger side of Daniel's pick-up. "Let's move so we aren't around so many people. Maybe sit further back on the outskirts of the crowd."

"Sounds good." Sarah and Whiskey trailed after Jared as he walked toward an area where people often ran their dogs.

Ginger and Daniel joined them a few minutes later after Sarah had spread a big blanket and Whiskey was lying atop it while chowing down on his early dinner.

"I see someone is starving." Ginger laughed. She hugged Sarah hello as Daniel asked Jared how he liked his new desk.

"I can't wait to use it. I spent a few hours today unpacking and putting things away in the studio. It's almost set up." His eyes were lit up like a kid unwrapping his birthday presents.

"It was a beautiful gift," Daniel said, pulling an alcohol-free beer from his cooler. "Anyone else want one?"

"I'll try it," Jared said.

"None for me, thanks," Sarah said. "I'll have some wine." She pulled it from her bag and offered some to Ginger.

Just as Ginger was about to respond, Mayor Trish's voice resounded from the stage. "Good afternoon, Cottageville citizens. It's my pleasure to see so many of you here for our concert today. Our local chamber music group, The Fermata Collective, has asked two of our high school students to join them as they play Dvorak's String Quartet No. 12 in F Major, which is sometimes called "American" and was written right in our home state in the town of Spillville. I think this is perfect as we approach the Fourth of July. Join me now in welcoming The Fermata Collective, and special guests Julianna Chin and Bart Brahmin to the stage." Mayor Trish started to clap and everyone assembled joined her as the artists carried their instruments onto the stage and took their seats in a semicircle. The first violinist played a note and the others quickly tuned to her before she launched them into the first lively movement.

Jared unpacked the board of food and the condiments and passed around small plates and napkins as the others kept their eyes on the stage.

Ginger leaned close to Sarah's ear and whispered, "Think there will be another burglary this afternoon?" She glanced around at the hundreds of people in the park.

Sarah shrugged her shoulders and whispered, "Guess we'll know soon enough."

"Are you coming to our house on the Fourth of July?" Ginger asked, grabbing some salami, cheese, and olives from the board.

"Wouldn't miss it. What should we bring?"

"Yourselves, Whiskey. Whatever you want. We'll have stuff to grill so maybe a side or an appetizer."

"Do you prefer Johnnie Walker or Jack Daniel's?"

Eying Sarah inquisitively, Ginger asked, "What? Am I missing something?"

Sarah chuckled, "Never mind. How many people are you inviting?"

"Just Daniel's parents and you guys. Small. Low-key."

"Why not your parents?" Sarah asked. Ginger had grown up in Cottageville, though she went away for university and stayed away for a few years after that, before returning and opening Java and Juice.

"They are traveling. You know that big RV they bought earlier this year? They are driving up to Alaska. Last I heard, they were somewhere in the Canadian Rockies having the time of their lives."

"Oh good for them." Sarah put some food on her own plate, figuring she should eat and listen to music instead of carrying on a side conversation the whole time. She could see Robert Wise in the first row and center of the stage, sitting in his chair and swaying to the music. She was sure his face was beaming and he wore a wide grin.

A half hour later all four movements of Dvorak's piece were done and The Fermata Collective surprised the audience by opening the repertoire up to child-friendly requests. A blond haired kindergartener in the front row near Robert Wise yelled out, "Row, Row, Row Your Boat" and the quartet launched into the song, with the audience singing along. That was followed by "America the Beautiful" and "Bridge Over Troubled Water." When someone yelled out "Yellow Submarine," the group paused, conferred, and then played a rendition that had people on their feet swaying with their arms around each other and singing the chorus loudly, Sarah, Ginger, Daniel, and Jared, included. Whiskey parked himself on his butt and moved his head back and forth watching the people in front of them.

"It's amazing watching our town participate as one group," Jared said in Sarah's ear.

But it wasn't until the quartet surprised the crowd with their final song of the afternoon, "Bohemian Rhapsody" that everyone hushed, sat again, and looked to be in awe of those on the stage until the final B flat played. Then the concert goers went wild, jumping to their feet, clapping and whistling, giving the musicians a standing ovation.

"A bit more lively than a standing O at a baroque concert." Ginger grinned.

"And way more kid-friendly," Sarah said. "I love how they made this show for all ages."

An encore seemed to be out of the question as the musicians were climbing down the stairs near the stage and talking to people in the audience. Sarah saw the first violinist stop near the front row of people and squat down to a small child, who must have asked if she could touch the instrument as the woman was moving the girl's tiny fingers over the strings. Sarah smiled to herself at the kindness of her community.

She asked Ginger, "Was this town always so nice?"

"What do you mean?" Ginger asked. Daniel stood next to her and regarded Sarah as Jared packed up the leftovers.

"People here are nice. They care about their neighbors. Yes, sometimes it is too small town with everyone in everyone's business. But for the most part, it's nice. Was it always this way? You two grew up here."

"Yes, people care. And that's mostly a good thing," Ginger said. "But when we were young, I hated it. It was intrusive and felt like no matter what you did, good or bad or in-between, it would always get back to your parents."

Daniel chuckled. "I'll say. It was like having five hundred parents instead of just two."

"But on the other hand," Ginger said, "when I crashed on my bike, I knew I could run to the nearest house and be taken care of. No one was a stranger. Of course, there were fewer people then."

"But at its heart," Daniel added, "Cottageville hasn't changed too much since my parents grew up here. It's just gotten bigger and the Main Street shopping district is more blocks now."

"And it has a bit more crime, probably," Sarah said.

Daniel laughed. "It certainly has had some unexpected, spill-over issues the last few years. No place is immune to drugs and a bit of crime. And let's face it, Sarah," Daniel teased, "you like having puzzles to solve. You have a knack."

"Uhh, don't forget they often find me," Sarah protested.

Daniel raised his eyebrows but said nothing.

"It's true, but you're right. I do love a good mystery," Sarah admitted, before grinning at her friends.

"Are you Scooby Doo?" Ginger joked with Whiskey, who cocked his head to the side and moved his ears like satellite dishes tuning into a signal. "I don't think so. You're much smarter."

Whiskey gave Ginger a black lipped grin and raised his paw to slap her five.

"And so much funnier," she added.

Sarah shook her head at her dog's understanding.

"Okay, Watson," she said. "Get your butt off the blanket so I can fold it and we can go home." To her BFF and Daniel she said, "I'm so glad you suggested this. It was fun. Let's do it again next week." And then she gave them both hugs.

CHAPTER 6

The next morning, Whiskey beelined to Bill's on the morning walk. Sarah was surprised he didn't stop to mark many bushes or sniff any scents. He was a dog on a mission, and she jogged after him to keep up. Only when he was on the front porch did he stop, plop his butt on the wooden planks, and place two paws on Bill's knees. Whiskey's brown eyes gazed up at his friend's face. Bill sat at the wooden table with his coffee mug to his right and the *Courier* spread before him.

"Hey, bud." Bill scratched between Whiskey's ears. "I'm okay. Really I am. And thank you for alerting Sarah to my troubles."

Bill bent at the waist and touched his lips to Whiskey's snout before reaching into the treat container and pulling out not one but two beef dog biscuits. "You get an extra today for your good deed."

"That's generous of you," Sarah said. "We're so glad to see you sitting out here, able to continue with your routine. How do you feel?"

"I was tired yesterday, but today I feel like myself."

"That's wonderful," Sarah said.

"It is indeed." Bill rubbed Whiskey's ears.

"Hey, did Officer Beams or anyone else ask if you are missing anything from your house? I'm sure you've heard about the break-ins, and Janice said your doors are always unlocked."

"Chief James stopped by yesterday in the late afternoon. Mostly to check on my health, I believe. But he asked. Janice did a walk-thru Saturday night, she said, and then she locked up. When she and Glad brought me home, I looked, but nothing seemed to be disturbed. Of course, I'm not sure an old guy like me has much that others want." A chuckle rumbled through Bill's chest.

Sarah glanced up the street toward the Maslows' antique store, but she couldn't see much from where she stood since there was a house in between.

"Do you need anything?" Sarah asked. "Jared is bringing you some soup and biscuits and returning your chairs when he gets off work today."

"That's nice of him. Thank you. But no, Sarah. I'm good. Just keep bringing my favorite boy by my house in the mornings." He smiled down at Whiskey.

"Will do." Sarah leaned over and kissed Bill's forehead. "Take care of yourself. Come on, Whisk. We need to get to work."

They crossed the street and headed south half a block before Sarah pulled open the red door to Java and Juice. The bell above the door tinkled, and Mayor Trish sat at her usual table, but Barbara wasn't yet with her.

"Good morning, Sarah, Whiskey," the mayor greeted. "Have you figured out who robbed those places yet, Sarah?" A sparkle flashed in Trish's eyes as her cheeks bunched like a chipmunk with acorns, and she gave Sarah a mischievous smile.

"Not yet." Sarah beamed at her.

Since no one was in line, Whiskey marched himself right up the counter where Jared was manning the register. The dog looked up at his housemate and smiled, wanting to be acknowledged and given one of Ginger's homemade chicken dog biscuits.

"Slap me five," Jared commanded, leaning over the counter with his hand outstretched. Sarah preferred if Whiskey had to work a bit for his treats.

Whiskey raised his right paw and slapped Jared's hand.

"You rock." Jared tossed him the treat, which Whiskey caught in the air.

"Mi'lady, what can I get you?" Jared reached for Sarah's to-go tumbler and turned to fill it with black coffee.

"My lord," Sarah curtsied, in the funny schtick they had done since way before they became a couple. "Two of those blueberry scones with the red, white, and blue drizzle and what's the salad of the day?"

"Ginger created a colorful and flavorful blackberry peach salad with chicken breast chunks and honeyed ricotta. You and Em should have that."

"Ooo yum. Yes that. Thank you."

Jared turned to grab the pre-made salads from the cooler, rang up the total, and Sarah tapped her card adding a healthy tip. Jared leaned across the counter and gave her a quick kiss. "Love you."

"You too," Sarah said, taking the bag of food from him.

On her way to the door, she asked Mayor Trish and Barbara, who had just entered the cafe, "Were any places robbed during yesterday's concert?"

Trish eyed Barbara like she didn't know the answer, and Barbara shook her head. "Not that I know about. But James took the day off since he was in a use it or lose it PTO situation." She shrugged.

"You guys really need a vacation," Trish said.

"Don't need to tell me twice," Barbara said.

"We can keep Sascha for you," Sarah volunteered, before wondering if she should have asked Jared before offering. She was still adjusting to having someone else living in her house 24/7 and considering their needs.

"Oh Sarah, that's so kind of you to offer," Barbara said. "Sascha would love to spend more time with Whiskey, but with the uptick in crime this past year or two, James thinks his presence is too important to leave for too many days in a row."

"That's rubbish," Trish said. "His officers are capable of handling anything that happens. Tell him I'm ordering him, as his boss, to take you somewhere." Then she cackled like it was the funniest thing she ever said.

Barbara laughed right along with her.

Sarah excused herself and Whiskey, and they exited the cafe.

They walked a few blocks south and then took a left to cross Main Street and traveled another half block down Rosewood Drive to the green door of Carter's Canine Coiffure. The lights were on inside and Sarah's assistant, Emily Colt, age twenty, was placing nail clippers and scissors and trimmers at their work stations. She wore a denim dog print apron over a torn and faded denim mini skirt and black Wonder Woman t-shirt. Black Doc Marten boots adorned her feet. Emily's dyed black hair was gathered atop her head in black bow and a red, white, and blue flag had been stenciled in paint across the back of her head.

"Cool hair," Sarah said, though Emily always had a creative and edgy 'do.

"Thanks. Travis will be here soon with Sean and Sophia." Travis and Emily had become an official couple a few months before, once Emily had decided to completely friend-zone Taylor, a pale Johnny Depp in *Edward Scissorhands* look alike twenty-year-old gamer who worked part-time for Ginger at Java and Juice and lived with an iguana named Iggy. Travis was a few years older and was an assistant to Sergio, Cottageville's answer to the high-end hairdresser.

It was usual for Travis to pick up the shelties from their grooming appointments but not to drop them off first thing in the morning so Sarah asked, "Where's Sergio?"

"At a hair convention in New York. Travis house and sheltie-sat all weekend."

A bit of color infused into Emily's cheeks causing Sarah to smile and tease. "And you did, too?"

"Not the whole weekend. I helped with walks and things. They are such cute dogs."

Sarah knew they weren't the only thing that Emily thought was cute, but she let it go. "I got us festive blueberry scones for breakfast." She pulled the food out of the bag and put it on a table in the back before putting the salads in the refrigerator. The Coiffure had once been someone's home, but Sarah had combined some of the spaces so that the front door opened into a waiting area with chairs and a sofa, a big counter with a hinged part separated it from the grooming area—which used to be the kitchen and dining room—where there were steel tables sporting poles alongside with leather loops to hold a dog's head, and stainless steel wash bins lined the wall, some at waist height and one at the ground level that was walk-in. Shelves of products and towels stacked neatly were anchored to the wall above the tubs.

The backrooms of the Coiffure consisted of a full bathroom, a breakroom, and a room stacked with dog crates that no one ever used. All dogs that came for grooming were well-behaved, except for Chutney the chihuahua, and a cage would do nothing to curb her Tasmanian Devil style behavior.

Sarah slid her own denim dog-print apron over her head and double-wrapped it around her waist just as the front door of the Coiffure opened and Whiskey ran to greet Sean and Sophia. Dressed in a black button down shirt and black jeans with black loafers—the official uniform of Sergio's salon—Travis trailed behind the shelties, who strained at their leashes to jump on their cattle dog friend. Whiskey lay on the ground and let them crawl over him before standing, shaking, and encouraging them to chase him as he ran under the hinged part of the counter and into the grooming area.

Travis let go of the leather leashes, and they snaked after the dogs.

"Hi, Travis," Sarah said. "Does he want the usual? Nail trim, anal glands expressed, baths, and bandanas?"

"Yes. And he said Sophia's been a bit itchy so if you have something for that..."

"We do indeed. We'll use it on both dogs."

"Thanks." Travis' eyes roamed from Sarah to Emily, who was bent down and removing the leashes from Sean and Sophia. "Nice to see you, Em."

She stood up and grinned at him. "You, too. It's your last day of freedom," she joked.

"Sergio returns today?" Sarah asked.

"Tonight," Travis said. Sergio had a reputation for being meticulous—okay, a total perfectionist—whether it was in his salon, the way he dressed, or pretty much in every aspect of his life. That obsession to detail made him the top of his trade—and also the priciest in the area. But let's just say, his OCD often made working with him a nightmare.

"So it's a good thing his housekeeper comes today," Travis said cryptically, before adding, "not that we messed anything up or anything. But you know. Dog hair and all that." He shrugged. "Text me when they are ready. Thanks. Bye, Em." He flashed her a smile that went all the way to his eyes, which Sarah imagined with protruding hearts popping from them like a cartoon character. The thought amused her but she kept it to herself.

Hiding her smirk, Sarah scooped up Sean and set him into the wash tub while Emily snagged Sophia. Whiskey stood between the two tubs watching his friends get soaked. They didn't look very happy about it.

As Emily squeezed a dollop of medicated shampoo onto her palm, she asked, "So, Sarah, what do you make of the burglaries? The Cottageville online message board had all kinds of speculation. Someone said it was, and I quote, 'damn teenagers.' Someone else suggested it was well-planned by professional thieves. Is that even a thing, Sarah? Professional thieves?"

Sarah scrubbed Sean's back with her fingers and the dog leaned into the massage. "Isn't that what the guys in the *Ocean* numbered movies are, professional thieves, and in *The Italian Job,* too?"

"I guess. But we're in Cottageville. Not somewhere with high stakes or high grab values like Vegas." Emily pursed her red painted lips.

"True," Sarah said. "Any other speculation?"

Emily started to rinse Sophia, who shook as the water hit her spine, spraying water in a three-foot radius. Sarah laughed as water dripped from Emily's nose and her own. "Oh, the hazards of dog grooming," Em said.

"Water is innocuous compared to bites and scratches," Sarah said.

"Truth. The only other speculation was that maybe the antique store was the target and the other places were broken into to divert attention from that."

Sarah's eyes went wide. "That's an interesting thought. You've lived here all of your life. Do you know the Maslows?"

Emily shrugged one shoulder. "I know who they are and say hi when I see them. They are older than my parents. Their oldest daughter may have babysat me a long time ago once or twice, but I don't really remember her. And I've only been in their store once, when I was a kid and my mom was looking to buy a replacement lamp for a set my grandma had. My grandpa bumped into the end table in the dark one night, and it crashed to the ground and its glass base broke."

"Did the speculator about the antique store being the target say why?" Sarah wrapped Sean in a big towel and carried the bundled sheltie to the grooming table.

"No. Though someone posted maybe Marcus or whatever his name is that was helping out while they were gone staged the robbery."

"Why on earth would he do that?" Sarah asked.

"They didn't say. You know those forums. It's a lot of haters and trash talkers because they can remain mostly anonymous."

Sarah rolled her eyes at Emily. "I'll never get the haters gonna hate b.s. Takes as much energy... maybe more ...to hate than to be kind. Why can't we just get along, people?"

"We can, Sarah. We do." Emily quipped, flashing her a grin. "But not everyone can be like your cattle dog." Whiskey stood on his hind legs with his front paws on the grooming table that Sean sat upon. The cattle dog was straining upward, trying to assure his smaller friend that everything would be okay as Sarah toweled him off and then turned on the blow dryer.

CHAPTER 7

After Travis had picked up the Shetland sheepdogs and two other dogs had had shampoos and trims, Sarah and Emily sat at the table and ate their salads.

"Mmm. This is so good, Sarah. I love the unexpected tanginess of the green olives and how it offsets the fruitiness of the rest of the salad," Emily said. She scrolled on her phone as she forked bits of food into her mouth.

"Ginger certainly has a winner on her hands. Any plans for July fourth?" It was in a week and because it fell on a Monday, it meant they would have a three-day weekend, though Sarah and Emily did work two Saturday half-days each month, but not this coming weekend.

"Travis and Taylor and I and some other friends will be in the park for the fireworks. Other than that, nothing much. What about you?"

"Jared, Whiskey, and I have been invited to Ginger and Daniel's for a cookout with his parents. We'll probably be in the park for the fireworks, too."

"They don't bother Whiskey?"

Sarah shook her head no. "He's calm around loud noises and motorcycles and delivery trucks. Unlike this girl I knew in college, her dog Casper would go absolutely nuts around loud noises, big trucks, or even the mailman. Casper must have had quite a history before she adopted him."

"Oh, wow, the poor thing. It's a good thing Whiskey is so chill."

"Most definitely. Lots of pets need sedatives and don't like to be alone on July fourth, and it's cruel to make them be. Some are terrified. I know of another dog who used to curl into a ball under a desk with his back up against a wall. He acted like a war veteran with PTSD any time a firework boomed. It was so sad to see."

Just then sirens wailed and Emily and Sarah could hear first responder vehicles beeping and speeding half a block away up Main Street. "I wonder what's going on," Sarah said.

"Last time there was an accident on the state route," Em said.

"Or there was that kind of racket when that kid put the smoke bomb in the toilet of the school and someone thought it was an actual explosive," Sarah reminded.

"That was epic." Emily grinned.

"The principal didn't think so."

"True." Emily typed some things into her phone and paused. "People on the message board are asking what all of the sirens are about. " She scrolled a bit and squinted at her phone. Sarah assumed she was reading the responses because Emily finally said, "No one seems to know for sure but someone posted the address given over the police scanner and said it was a medical emergency." She frowned at the screen. "Do you know who lives out there?" She pushed her phone at Sarah.

Sarah was looking at a Google Maps image of the street. "I don't think so." She zoomed in more on the map. "It isn't that far from Ginger's, maybe a mile or two."

"I guess we'll find out soon enough," Emily said, eating her last bite of salad. "Nothing stays a secret here for long."

The green door of the Coiffure opened and Emily disposed of her to-go container on her way to greet their latest customer, though she was seconds behind Whiskey, who was crouching playfully with his butt in the air in front of Coco Chanel the corgi and her human Braidington Bagley.

Sarah was right behind Emily, and when she saw who it was, she prayed she didn't have food stuck between her teeth. Braidington was the best looking man in Cottageville as far as Sarah and a lot of the population with ovaries were concerned. He had wiry black, close-cropped hair, melted milk chocolate eyes, a jawline that could cut glass, and a smile like Lucien Laviscount. He was tall—around six-three, Sarah guessed,—worked out, and often wore expensive suits, fitting for his lawyer and money manager occupation. But he was off limits to his female admirers since for a month shy of a year, he had been in a relationship with police officer John Beams.

Braidington squatted and scooped up his spoiled girl and placed her on the counter in front of Emily. He kissed her head between her ears. "You be good and let these nice ladies give you a bath. I'll be back for you in a bit," he said to his dog.

"Is two hours good?" Sarah asked.

Braidington glanced at his Rolex. "It should be. Might be two and a half. I have a Zoom meeting with a client."

"No problem," Sarah said, as Emily carried Coco Chanel back to a tub.

"Thank you, Sarah." He pivoted on his black loafers and took his royal blue suited self out the door, got into his black BMW M8 Gran Coupe, and drove away.

Sarah asked, mostly to herself, but also to Em, "How is it possible that I never get tired of looking at him?"

Emily snorted, her voice echoing off the tiled wall. "Because he looks like a walking Calvin Klein ad and smells like cedarwood dreams. That kind of thing doesn't get old."

Sarah leaned against the counter, gazing out the window after his taillights. "Even knowing he's gay doesn't take the shine off."

"Unattainable men are the safest kind to crush on...well that and celebrities," Emily said, while running her fingers into the corgi's wet fur. "You get all of the fantasy and none of the drama."

"Yep. But now I'm going to spend the next two and half hours wondering if I actually said 'two hours' or just made some weird gurgling noise."

Emily laughed. "Pretty sure he didn't notice. He's all about Ms.

Chanel. Treats her like she's the queen's favorite corgi."

"She's definitely his," Sarah replied as the green Coiffure door opened again and Kai Tanaka, owner of Cottageville's only martial arts temple, and his Shibu inu Momo walked in side by side. "Hey, Kai." Sarah opened the hinged counter and stepped through, following Whiskey who ran to greet Momo, who stood shorter but had the same coloring as the cattle dog. "I have Momo for a nail trim but does he need anything else?"

"If you have time to bathe and brush him, that would save me the hassle. He's been shedding so much this summer."

"Many of my canine clients have been doing that since it's been extra warm. We have some wiggle room in our schedules today so if you can give us two hours..." Sarah's voice trailed off.

Kai looked at his smartwatch and said two hours was good as the summer camp he ran was over for the day and his afternoon classes didn't start until four.

"Perfect. See you around two-thirty then." Sarah led Momo to one of the wash tubs and picked him up, put him inside, and turned on the water. A gentle shampoo was at the ready on the shelf above her head. Shibus were a breed that weren't washed often as washing could strip their coat of the natural oils needed for their built-in heating and cooling system.

An hour later, when Coco Chanel was done and curled into a ball in the waiting room with Whiskey, Emily took a break and played on her phone. "Hey, Sarah, you know those sirens we heard?"

"Yeah." Sarah ran a brush through Momo's tail one last time. She had gotten most of the loose fur out of his double-coats and had cleaned out the brush at least half a dozen times during his grooming.

"Someone wrote on the message board that it was in response to a shooting of that old guy we were talking about earlier, Micas Brighton."

Sarah's head snapped up to Emily. "What? Somebody shot him?"

"That's what somebody posted in response to 'Why were there a lot of sirens?'Anyone know what is going on?' from CTGVL6."

"Why would someone shoot a retired historian?" The words flew out of Sarah's mouth before she realized how stupid they sounded. Why did anyone shoot someone else? Money. Greed. Jealousy. Hatred. It was justifiable in some people's minds for a lot of reasons. "Did he die?"

Em's finger repeatedly slid up on her phone's screen, scrolling through the messages. She frowned. "It doesn't say."

"I wonder if he called nine-one-one himself or if someone found him. It isn't like his neighbors live that close."

"True, but a gunshot can be loud." Emily's eyes narrowed like she was deep in thought, and then she said, "Hey, Sarah, don't you think it is weird that he was filling in for the Maslows while they had a break-in and not even two days later he gets shot? Seems like one hell of a coincidence."

"But other places were robbed, too. Daphne Smith's house was one of them."

Emily's eyes went wide and her mouth formed an o. "You don't think someone shot people at each of the places, do you?" She grimaced like the thought was too much.

"No. That would be ludicrous. And besides, didn't you say he was shot at his house? His house wasn't robbed. Or at least I don't think it was." Sarah placed Momo on the floor as he was all clean and maybe one pound lighter from removed loose fur. "I'm going to pull up and re-read a couple of newspaper articles about the break-ins and see if we can pinpoint exactly where each was, and maybe start a list of what was stolen. There's got to be a connection or pattern or something." Sarah sat at the table in front of her laptop.

"Okay. While you do that, I'll scour the message board and see what I can find. It looks like we've another mystery to solve, Sarah." Enthusiasm oozed from Emily like honey on a hot biscuit—slow, sticky, and impossible to ignore.

But just as they got started in their searches, a black Ford Explorer, with a big St. Bernard head poking from the open passenger window, pulled in front of the Coiffure. The dog was white and dark chocolate brown and had strings of saliva hanging from his jowls.

"Sebastian's here," Emily said as Coco Chanel, Whiskey, and Momo raced to the door, tails lashing behind them except for Coco.

"Last dog of the day," Sarah said. The St. Bernard was easiest washed and groomed if two people attended to him at once. But, he was a notorious shaker and sprayed everything in a six-foot radius so Sarah preferred to groom him at the end of the day.

"Move out of the way," Sarah commanded to the three dogs at the door, as she slowly scooted it open. "Hi, Scott. Sebastian, here let me wipe your face." Sarah moved the towel in her hand to the dog's mouth to wipe the drool. Sebastian's human was Scott Simon and his salt and pepper hair was cut close to his scalp, which once again reminded Sarah of a closely groomed Kerry blue terrier.

"Oh thanks, Sarah. It's hard to stay on top of it. The whole side of my ride is decorated in Sebastian slobber. Isn't it, boy?" He affectionately scratched his dog's neck. When he noticed the other three dogs vying for his attention, he said, "Busy day today, huh?"

"Steady, but not too bad," Sarah responded. "Can you return at five? Come on, big boy, let's give you a bath."

"I'll be here," Scott promised. He said goodbye to the three smaller dogs and saw himself out.

"If you promise not to shake, we'll give you a rawhide," Emily said to Sebastian as she led him back to the walk in tub.

"I'm not sure bribes are in his vocabulary," Sarah said.

"Whiskey seems to understand them," Emily said, as he followed her and Sebastian. Coco Chanel trailed after him as fast as her short legs could take her. Momo ignored them and jumped onto the waiting room sofa and parked his butt on it, sitting upright like a human. He stared at the door like he was willing Kai to return.

But Braidington beat him to it. As he paid, Sarah asked what he and John were doing for July fourth. "At the moment, I don't know." His eye shifted right and left and then he lowered his voice and said, "He was first on scene for this afternoon's shooting and is taking the lead. Pretty sure it's a murder so our plans are dashed, and he may be working the holiday weekend."

"Oh that sucks. But wait...does that mean Micas didn't make it? I'm glad to know John's on the case," Sarah said.

"No. He was gone before they arrived. That's all I know." And then he surprised Sarah by raising his hand to his lips and pulling a proverbial zipper across them.

Sarah mimicked his gesture. He turned and carried his corgi out the door.

CHAPTER 8

When Sarah and Whiskey entered their house a few minutes after six p.m. they were greeted by the scent of roasted chicken. Whiskey's nose was in the air and twitched, and he chased after the scent as fast as his legs would let him. "Something smells delicious," Sarah said as she entered the kitchen. "Do I have time for a quick shower to wash the day's dander away?"

She stood on her toes and pressed a kiss to Jared's lips and not just because he was wearing a black apron emblazoned with words in white: KISS THE CHEF over his tan shorts and navy blue t-shirt.

"Ten minutes. I'll feed my furry BFF in the meantime."

"Thank you." Sarah stole a cherry tomato from the pile Jared was halving and popped it into her mouth. "So good. Tastes like summer."

"It also is." Jared grinned, swatting her butt as she moved past him on the way to their bedroom.

Six minutes later, with her hair wet and wearing shorts and a tank top with "cattle dog mom" on the chest, Sarah set the table and Jared brought the food into the dining room: herb roasted whole chicken, au gratin potatoes, and a green salad with a berry poppy seed dressing. After a few bites of food, Jared said, "My publisher called today and you'll never guess why."

"You've hit another bestseller list?" Sarah took a sip of water.

"Nope."

"They've moved up the publication date of your second book and want it now instead of the fall?"

"Not even close."

Sarah eyed him and tried to read his mind, but it felt as impenetrable as granite.

He flashed her a dimple. "Give up?"

"Contract for more books than the sequel?"

Jared shook his head from side to side.

"Chinese language rights? Mandarin? Cantonese?"

"Already sold those."

"Oh." Sarah knew Jared's book had been translated into eighteen languages, but she didn't know which ones. "Umm, because it is doing so well they called to say it is going into a second printing?"

"No. At least not yet." He forked some potato and put it into his mouth.

"Um, you're getting a new editor? Don't they often jump from place to place?"

"Sometimes, I believe, especially the younger ones. But no, that wasn't what the call was about."

"They sold film rights to Hollywood?" Sarah's eyes sparkled dreamily. "And Jemma Ortega has signed to be the female lead?"

"I wish," Jared said.

"Me too." Sarah ate another bite of chicken before saying, "Okay. I'm out of ideas. Tell me."

"Well, you know how I told you that readers in the Czech Republic just love my book and my art? It's the place where I get the most love."

"Yep. You've mentioned that. You've been a guest on a few podcasts there and didn't some gallery in Prague ask if you wanted to do an art exhibit?"

Jared's huge smile lit up his face like a firework exploding. "Yes, and I'm still working out the details on that. I'd love to do it."

"You should. I'll go with you for the opening. I'm sure Whiskey would love to spend time with Ginger and Daniel or maybe Em would be willing to stay here with him."

"That would be awesome." He reached across the table and squeezed her hand. "So my publisher called to say the truck carrying cases of my books from the printers to the distribution center was hijacked a few weeks ago. They didn't tell me at first because the police thought it was a mistake, like the thieves thought something else was in the truck. But then, they started seeing copies of the book show up on the black market and people selling them on the streets. The publisher said the book has become hotter than cryptocurrency.

People can't get enough. So they are actually printing more there and having armored cars and guards deliver them to the distribution center and to stores. Can you believe that?" Jared couldn't contain his excitement. He bounced in his chair and his face beamed like the sun. "That's almost better than winning an award or making the bestseller's lists."

"That's crazy. I'm so happy for you. What an honor to have work so in demand people want to steal it." Sarah laughed hard, sounding a bit like a hyena. And then she sobered up. "Jared, do you think people in foreign countries might counterfeit your work? I mean with all of the technology, it could be easy to do and some printer we know nothing about could print it and a foreign publisher could claim rights and sell a million copies and you'd never see a dime." The thought troubled Sarah. She put down her fork and stared at the love of her life. "Do you think that could happen?"

"Almost anything is possible." Jared looked into her eyes. "There are shady people everywhere who try to scam people. But I'm sure my publisher's legal team pays attention to things like that...or at least I'd think they would." He frowned. "But you know, I've never asked them about that and I probably should. Plenty of patented products have been ripped off, produced, and sold in our country and in others before crackdown happens."

"I'd hate for that to happen to you." Sarah patted his hand.

"Me too. And you can be sure that in the next interviews I do, I'm going to tell the Czech Republic story. I mean how cool is that? Not too many artists or authors can say the same."

A vague memory was working its way to the front of Sarah's mind, and she suddenly had a vision of the iconic paper mache caterpillar in her head. "Actually, you're in the same company as Eric Carle. I read an article a long time ago that something very similar happened to him during the translation and shipping of *The Very Hungry Caterpillar*, except it was maybe in Poland...I can't remember the exact country and all of the details. But you might be able to find it online."

"Eric Carle was my hero as a kid. I loved his books."

"Hey, not to change the subject but I am. Did you hear that Micas Brighton was shot and killed today?"

"Someone mentioned a shooting and we heard the sirens, but I didn't know who or what was shot."

"You know who he is, right?"

"Older guy. Einstein-y hair? Was a professor or worked at a museum or something? I don't think he's lived here long, right?"

"Maybe a couple or few years. I met him twice, I think, in passing. No real discussions, but I always heard he was a historian. Though I don't know what his speciality area is...or was." Sarah frowned.

"But he helped out at the antique store. We know that." Jared ate the last bite of salad from his plate. "Need second servings of anything?" He raised his eyebrows with the question.

"Nah. I'm good. It was all delicious. Thank you for spoiling me by making dinner so often."

"My pleasure. Thank you for providing a rent-free roof over my head." His dimple indented again.

"Anyway," Sarah said. "I'm curious how a retired historian or whatever he is or was ends up shot in his own home."

"Home invasion? Disturbed a robber? Someone shot at a deer and hit him instead?" Jared raised his eyebrows at her. "Could be any reason or no reason at all. But it sounds like Sleuth Sarah wants to be on the case." He chuckled. "And since Whiskey and I are your trusty sidekicks, what would you like us to do?"

"Nothing yet. But tonight I want to do some internet research and see if I can find out anything about Micas Brighton, where he lived before here, where he worked, if he has family, and if he is—i mean, was—a historian or professor, I'd love to understand what his area was and if he wrote any papers or books or anything that could make sense of the shooting." Sarah stood and stacked their empty plates, starting to clear the table.

"Because you don't think it was random?"

Sarah shrugged. "I don't know. But I think it is very suspect that there was a break-in at a store he was minding and then two days later he turns up dead. To misquote Shakespeare, 'There's something fishy in the small town of Cottageville.'"

"And you want to figure out what it is." Jared followed her into the kitchen with the chicken platter and potatoes. After putting them on the counter, he wrapped his arms around her. "Have I told you how much I love your inquisitive mind?" He kissed the tip of her nose.

Sarah smiled at him.

After cleaning up the kitchen and putting away the leftovers, Sarah pulled her laptop from her backpack and sat with it on the sofa. Jared settled next to her and flipped through the options on Netflix and then Amazon Prime before he switched back to Netflix. "Are you okay if I watch a wood carving competition while you poke around the net?" Whiskey lay perpendicular to them on the love seat with his eyes closed. Occasionally one of his paws would twitch as if he was running in his dreams.

"Absolutely." Sarah debated whether she should type Micas' name into a browser to see what popped up or if she should start with LinkedIn or Academia.edu or another site more specialized. But then she figured if he was in any of those places, they would appear in a browser search, so she went to her favorite browser and typed in the guy's name, thanking the naming gods his first name was spelled a bit unusual.

At the top of the list were Micas Brighton's articles written and published in academic and professional journals that spanned pre-Internet to the present. Topics included ways to authenticate sculptures and paintings; art techniques of various centuries; studies on the creations of specific artists who worked in bronze, marble, and other mediums; and even an article on some of the best known forgers in the nineteenth and twentieth centuries.

Sarah spent two hours reading what she could and taking notes on a legal pad while Jared watched four episodes of the wood carving show before saying he needed to go to bed. Morning would come too early.

"I'll be in soon," Sarah said. Her neck was sore from leaning in a very unergonomic way over the computer on her lap so she stretched it from side to side and then tilted her chin up as far as it would go. She shut the lid on the laptop and put it and the pad and pen on the coffee table.

"Come on, boy," Sarah said to Whiskey. "Last call time." She followed him to the back door, and once it was open, he bolted down the steps, ran ten feet into the grass, and then squatted a bit with his right leg lifted. As soon as he finished, he ran back inside and directly into the bedroom and onto the bed, where he put his head on Sarah's pillow and he stretched out his body and touched Jared's back with his feet.

"You're too funny," Sarah said. "As soon as I finish brushing my teeth, you're going to have to move."

He acknowledged her with his eyes but nothing more.

When she emerged from the bathroom, she forced him to move over...which meant Whiskey ended up between her and Jared with his head on the edges of both of their pillows, and he rested on his back with his paws in the air, where he sighed and closed his eyes.

Sarah knew when she had been bested, so she turned onto her left side and turned off the light on the nightstand.

CHAPTER 9

Sarah and Whiskey arrived at the Coiffure the next morning earlier than usual. Her laptop was in a bag over her shoulder and her hand clutched a Java and Juice bag of goodies—more of those red, white, and blue drizzled scones and chipotle lime chicken salads for lunch—and her tumbler filled with black coffee. Sarah was determined to dig into the robberies and murder-mystery before the day's appointments began. Whiskey must have been tired from his two morning walks as he curled into a ball in the back corner of the Coiffure to nap as soon as they got there.

Emily arrived ten minutes later with her hair styled and painted the same as the day before. She wore a short, red t-shirt dress with her combat boots. Half a buttered bagel was clenched between her teeth and a black folder was being held by her arm against her body. She plopped the folder on the front counter. "Morning," she mumbled around the bagel.

For once, Whiskey didn't run to her in greeting.

"What's with the bagel?" Sarah asked. "I brought you another blueberry scone."

"My stomach didn't want to wait. It wanted food an hour ago." Emily's teeth tore a bigger than bite size chunk from the bagel, which was studded with chunks of onion. After she chewed and swallowed, she added, "Don't worry. I have room for both," before flashing Sarah a grin. She looked around for Whiskey and spotted him in the corner, white tipped tail curled around his body. "He looked like a fox," she remarked.

Sarah broke off a piece of her scone and popped it into her mouth. "Yes, he does. And he's as wily as one, too. Anything new on the message board last night? Did you have time to check?"

"I did have time. Nothing new that wasn't conjecture or conspiracy. Someone swears there were two shots, or at least that they heard a second shot. Others told them it was probably a car backfiring." Emily ate the last bite of bagel and moved to the table on which Sarah had set Emily's scone.

"Interesting," Sarah said, pulling the strap of her paw-print apron over her head. "I wonder who is right."

"No idea." Emily pulled a piece of paper from the black folder. "I printed a map of Cottageville and thought maybe you could check with Officer Beams or Officer Grimes to find out the addresses where the robberies were and we could plot them on the map. I already put a star where Micas Brighton's house is." Emily pointed to a gold foil star that was illuminated by the overhead can lights.

"Is there still no information on the message group about which places were robbed? People talk so much in this town, you'd think we'd already know."

Emily tied her apron strings around her waist. "We know the antique store and Daphne Smith and then that guy who was quoted in the *Courier.*"

"But I don't know where he lives. Do you?" Sarah asked. She put an x on Main Street to indicate the Maslows' store.

"No. That's why I figured we'd need the addresses from an official source." Emily's brown eyes sparkled and her lips were in a bit of a smirk.

"Well I'm not sure the police would give me, a civilian, official information like the names of people who have been robbed and their addresses. Daphne's address is in our customer database. You look there for that," Sarah said, "and I'm going to check with Bill and Janice and see if they know who else was robbed or where the guy who was quoted in the newspaper who had the coin collection lives. He clearly has no pets as we've never met him." Sarah prided herself on knowing all of the canines' human companions as the Coiffure was the only grooming salon in a thirty-mile radius.

"Okay," Emily said, leaning over Sarah's laptop and clicking open the scheduling software.

Sarah pulled her phone from her pocket to call Bill, but the front door of the Coiffure opened and Whiskey raced to do his welcoming committee of one duties. Nine-year-old Bobby Davis shuffled in wearing a dirty shirt that looked like he had rolled in a sandbox. His t-shirt had horizontal stripes and his khaki shorts came to his knees. His arms encircled his originally white Bichon frise, which was now covered in a layer of dust. Bobby carried the dog against his chest and stomach. "Hey, Bobby. How's your summer going? I'm sure French Fry is glad to have you home all day every day."

"He is, Sarah. We go to the park and play in my yard. He likes to go everywhere I go." Love beamed from Bobby's blue eyes and the smile that created apples in his full, freckled cheeks.

"Does he like to play ball?" Emily asked, coming through the hinged counter to greet their youngest human customer.

"Sometimes. He loves to bite his stuffed dinosaur and shake it. It's so funny to watch his head shake and his ears flop."

"I'm sure it is. Whiskey does that with toys sometimes, too." Sarah consulted their schedule as Em took French Fry from Bobby. "I have him down for a bath and nail trim. Is that right?"

Bobby bobbed his head up and down. "His nails are sharp. When I picked him up yesterday, I got scratched." He held up his arm and pointed to a three-inch light red line crusted into his freckled skin.

"Did you wash that well?" Sarah asked.

"My mom did."

"That's good. Bobby, do you want to wait while we give him a bath or would you like to come back later."

Bobby looked down at his blue tennis shoe and then looked up at Sarah. "I'll wait." He climbed onto the sofa and looked down at his hands. "My mum is working today."

Sarah knew Bobby's mum worked part-time at the Cottageville library and that his dad drove trucks for one of the bigger farms in the area. Bobby was an only child and his dog was his best friend.

"You didn't want to sit through storytime at the library while you wait?" Sarah asked.

"Nah. Storytime is for babies." He picked at the skin near his thumb.

Whiskey must have sensed Bobby's loneliness that Sarah felt too because the cattle dog jumped onto the sofa, circled once, and then sat next to Bobby and put his head on the boy's thigh.

Bobby giggled. "You're a funny dog, Whiskey. And so soft." He pet the fur around Whiskey's neck and stroked his pointed ears.

Sarah watched them for a beat before turning back to the grooming area where Emily had the water going and French Fry looked like a frothy cloud with black eyes and a wagging tail.

"Sarah," Bobby said. "I saw you at the movies and then the ambulance came. Me and French Fry and Mum and Dad were there. When we got home, Dad said someone had been in our house." Bobby's eyes were as wide as a toddler's seeing his first snow fall.

"Did they take anything?" Sarah took a few steps toward Bobby and knelt down to his level as he and Whiskey still sat on the sofa.

"You mean like steal?"

"Yes."

"It's not nice to steal."

"That's right, Bobby, it isn't nice to steal. Did someone steal something from your house?"

Bobby nodded his head up and down, his eyes still wider than usual.

Sarah gave him a second to see if he'd say what on his own. After a few beats he said, "Not my stuff though."

"But something from your dad or mum?"

He nodded his head again. "Dad's wedding ring. He don't wear it much, cept to church. Me mum's earrings."

"Only those two things?" Sarah asked.

"Yea."

"Bobby, what's your address?"

Sarah knew he lived maybe three or five blocks from the Coiffure, down Main Street a block or two and then a left. But she wasn't sure of exactly which street or house.

"Three three seven Pansy Lane," Bobby said. "That's my house."

Sarah made a quick note in her phone of the address before asking, "Were you scared?"

Bobby's brow squished as he eyed Sarah suspiciously. "No. Why would I be scared?"

"Because someone was in your house." Sarah's voice was low and calm.

"Nah. They weren't there when we were. I didn't see them." He shrugged.

"That's good, Bobby. I'm glad you weren't home. And I'm glad none of your things were taken."

"Yeah. Mum wasn't too happy. She cried. But I told her I'd get her more earrings."

"You're a good son." Sarah ruffled his reddish-blond crew cut and gave him a big smile. "She's lucky to have you. Your dad, too."

"French Fry, too," he declared.

"You're right. French Fry, too. He's a very lucky dog. And he loves you very much."

Emily had the blow dryer going and the Bichon was being fluffed into a cotton ball, exactly how her young companion liked her. Her white fur was once again bright and clean.

The Coiffure door opened again and Bobby, Sarah, and Whiskey's heads swiveled toward the newcomers, a white Maltese named Sunshine who was in bad need of a trim. Her silky hair dragged along the ground as she walked on her leash ahead of her human Celeste Ingram. Celeste's hair also needed a trim, and it had been overbleached so it looked straw like. Her sequined t-shirt sparkled above her white cropped pants and white leather sandals.

"Sorry, Sarah," she said upon entering. "I know it's been too long. I've let her become a mess. I've no excuse, but I'm praying you can help us. Sunshine is so much happier when she feels pretty. And well, look at her." She pointed at the dog with her chin.

Sarah agreed that the Sunshine was not living up to her name. Droopy would have been more apropos or Dingy, but she kept those thoughts to herself.

"Hello, Mrs. Ingram," Bobby said, while remaining on the sofa.

"Hello, Bobby. How are you today?"

"I'm fine, Mrs. Ingram. Waiting for French Fry to finish his bath. He's almost done." He pointed to where Emily had the dog on the table and was clipping the nails of his back right foot.

"Two more minutes," Em said.

Sarah scooped up the Maltese and carried her through the hinged part of the counter. Whiskey climbed down from the sofa and trailed after her. "Can you come back at ten-thirty or eleven?" she asked Celeste.

"Yes. And do you have a patriotic bow or ribbon? I love it when she has that single ponytail in the front. You do that so well."

"Thank you, Celeste. And yes, red, white, and blue we can do."

"Fabulous. Ta-ta for now," she said. "Bye, Bobby. Be good."

"I'm always good," Sarah heard Bobby mumble under his breath as she placed Sunshine in a wash tub. She smiled to herself.

Emily finished the final fluffing of French Fry's tail and then she asked, "Hey, Bobby, do you want a fireworks bandana around his neck or a red, white, and blue bow on his collar?"

Bobby grimaced. "French Fry is afraid of fireworks."

"Okay. So no bandana. What about a bow on his collar?"

Bobby got off the sofa and walked toward the counter, eyeing his dog. "Nah. He looks good the way he is. Don'tcha, boy?"

Emily grinned at Bobby, as she lifted French Fry from the grooming table and set him on the ground. The dog bounded across the floor as fast as a tumbleweed in a gale storm. His tail bounced with each leap until he crashed right into Bobby's bare legs.

Bobby's laughter filled the Coiffure as he lifted his dog to face-level and kissed his wet, black nose. He transferred the dog back to the floor with a "Wait here," while he reached into the front pocket of his shorts and pulled out some money, which he handed under the counter to Emily, since he wasn't quite tall enough to see her over the top unless he stood a few feet back.

"Are you going to the fireworks in the park?" Emily asked him.

"Hmm. I'm not sure. I like them. But French Fry doesn't. I don't want him to be by himself with the booms."

"You're right that it is kind of loud and can get scary for dogs and cats. Does he have a Thundershirt or something like that to help him relax?"

"What's a Thundershirt?" Bobby picked up his dog again and was idly stroking its side as he held the dog to his chest.

"It's the brand name of a shirt for pets that provides some feeling of them being held and makes them calmer in storms, during fireworks, and other times where there are loud noises."

"Can I use my own shirt and wrap it around him?"

"I'm not sure it would work the same. Those shirts are unique and made with a special comforting design."

Bobby's lips pursed together and his eyes squinted like he was thinking hard. Then he looked up at Em. "Do you have one?" he asked.

"I don't. But I don't have a dog or cat."

"Does Whiskey have a Thundershirt?"

"No. But Whiskey isn't afraid of thunder or fireworks or much of anything." At his name, Whiskey trotted to them to join the conversation.

Sarah, who was pulling Sunshine from the tub, said, "Bobby, I'll send a message to your mom and suggest a shirt for French Fry. That way you could maybe all enjoy the fireworks."

"Okay, Sarah. Thanks. Bye, Emily." And with that, Bobby walked out of the Coiffure.

"They are cuter than a box of bunnies wearing bow ties," Emily said as the door shut behind them.

"Someone's been watching too many baby animal reels," Sarah joked.

"Guilty as charged, and I don't regret a minute." Emily returned to her station to clean it and to prepare for their next client.

CHAPTER 10

Sarah knew Sascha, the Order's German shepherd, was on the afternoon schedule, but she figured Barbara Order would be bringing the police dog to her appointment since the Chief was busy with the burglaries and the shooting death. Her eyebrows shot to her auburn hairline when Chief James opened the green door at one o'clock on the dot. Exhaustion emanated from his pores. His uniform was wrinkled in a way Sarah had never seen. Whiskey ran to greet him and the gorgeous black and tan beast at the chief's side.

"Hey, Chief," Emily called. "Whiskey, bring your buddy here."

The cattle dog ran a circle around Sascha, and he nipped her lightly at the bottom of her leg, urging her toward Em.

Chief James chuckled at the dogs.

"I'm surprised to see you," Sarah admitted. "I figured you'd be neck deep in the investigation."

"I am. But Barb had an appointment with Sergio. He wouldn't accept a little thing like murder as a reason for her to cancel." Sarcasm oozed from him like juice from an overripe peach. The smile on his face did not reach his eyes. "She promised to stop by for Sascha on her way home from the salon."

"Okay. Or Whiskey and I can always drop her by if that's easier for you," Sarah offered.

Chief James rubbed his face with his hand. "Thank you, but that's unnecessary." He turned to leave when Sarah said, "Hey, Chief. Bobby was in here earlier and said his house was one of the ones that was robbed."

"Yes, it was."

Sarah set Sunshine down on the floor as the dog's grooming was done. She moved to their backroom table and grabbed the map and carried it to the counter. "Em and I were plotting out the burglaries and this gold star marks the home of Micas Brighton. We have Bobby's house, the antique store, and Daphne's but we don't know the other two locations." She paused hoping he'd fill in the blanks.

And he didn't let her down. He pointed to two points on the map. "Here and here."

Sarah made circles in red marker. "Thank you." She eyed what was a cluster on the map...all except for the location of Daphne Smith's house, which was in town, but on its southwest edge, three streets away. "Four of them are on or just off Main Street."

"Yes," Chief James said. "We noted that."

"But Daphne's house is the outlier."

"Yes."

"I wonder why that is," Sarah said more to herself than to anyone else.

"We don't know."

"Well, I'm sure you'll figure it out," Sarah said, still staring down at the map as if willing it to speak to her.

"I'm sure we will, too," Chief James said. "I've got to go, Sarah. Have a good afternoon."

"Thank you. You, too," she said automatically. Her brain was turning the information over in her head. Could the thieves have passed by Daphne's house on their way out of town? Did they live near her? Or did they start there and then work their way toward Main Street and north?

Once the Coiffure's door was closed, Sarah approached Emily, who had Sascha in a walk-in tub, the water cascading over her double-coat. Sarah held the map in front of Em and said, "Look at this. Four of the robberies are maybe in a half-mile radius."

Emily frowned at the map. "Except for Daphne's?" It was both a question and an exclamation.

"Yes."

"Could she have been targeted for a different reason?"

"Like what?"

"I don't know. Like maybe, these—" She pointed a wet finger towards the cluster of dots. "Were the intended locations, but whoever doesn't like Daphne or was jealous of her wardrobe or shoes or whatever so included her in the mix?"

"That seems juvenile."

"Well, we still don't know it wasn't. Think about it. What do we know was stolen? Two pieces of jewelry from Bobby's parents. A coat and three pairs of designer shoes. A coin collection and cash... It's so random." Emily poured shampoo into her palm and used her fingers to work it through Sascha's thick fur.

Sarah took the map back to the table so it didn't get wet, but she walked back to Em and helped her wash the dog. Whiskey sat near them for moral support. "It doesn't seem like professional thieves, right? I mean if stealing things was my job or only source of income, I'd go into a place and take everything of value. Money. All of the jewelry. Silver. Tools. Electronics. Right?"

"Yeah, Sarah, that's what I'm saying."

"The other thing that bugs me about this is the fact that it was four residences and an antique store. Why a mix of houses and a business? And why that particular business? Many antiques are heavy and bulky. They aren't things you can carry out the door unless you have a truck waiting."

"True," Emily said, "but we have no idea what was stolen from the store."

The wheels in Sarah's head were turning now and gathering momentum like a greyhound chasing a rabbit. "And the store's window was broken, but neither Bobby or Daphne mentioned anything being physically broken at their houses."

"Maybe their houses were more easily accessible, like they left windows open or doors unlocked. After all, it is summer and...well...we are a small trusting town."

"True. But I want to double check on that." While Emily towel dried Sascha, Sarah individually texted Daphne and Bobby's mother asking how the thieves entered their houses. And then she also texted Mrs. Maslow, congratulating her on her daughter's achievements, letting her know that she and Jared had discovered the broken window on their shop and called the police, and asking if it was okay for her and Whiskey to stop by after work today.

"Of course, Sarah," Mrs. Maslow texted. "We appreciate you keeping an eye on our business."

"We'll be there at five-thirty. You're open until six?" Sarah texted in return.

"Yes. See you then."

The Coiffure door opened and Spike, an eighty-plus pound chiseled-muscle pit bull and his equally ripped human Tony came into the waiting area. Whiskey sped to greet them, sliding on the smooth floor right into Spike, who remained firmly standing and licked Whiskey's ear.

Thirty-five-year old Tony owned what was becoming a chain of gyms called Big T's Fitness, and Sarah had heard a rumor that he had started a second company offering personal protection services and corporate security, but she wasn't sure if it was true. Today, he looked like the stereotypical CEO in a dark charcoal suit with a flash of red pocket square, a blinding white shirt, and shiny cap-toe black oxfords that look softer than a newborn's skin. "Hey, Big T. How's it going?" she asked.

"Sarah. Good to see you. Busy as always. Spike and I have a

photoshoot this evening as the sun sets so I want him looking his best. No bandanas, but if you have a solid color bow tie, we can put it on his collar."

"We do. Blue, red, green, black, or gold?"

Tony paused, and for a moment, Sarah could almost see the thoughts flicker behind his eyes before he finally said, "Black's probably best–it'll go with his gray and white fur."

"Sounds good. We can have him ready in an hour if that works for you."

Tony looked down at his oversized titanium watch. "I'm headed to a meeting with a potential client, but I should be done by then."

"Okay. See you before four," Sarah grabbed ahold of Spike's collar and led him to a walk-in tub. "Let's get you looking your most handsome, big boy," she said to the dog.

Just as she reached to turn on the water, Sarah's phone chimed with an incoming text. She pulled it from her apron pocket and looked at the screen. Rebecca Davis had responded, "Yes, we had two things stolen from our home on Saturday night. The thief came in through the unlocked front door, the police think."

Sarah texted, "Did you have other valuables besides the two things stolen?"

Three dots appeared as if Rebecca was writing so Sarah refrained from turning on Spike's bath water.

"Yes. Guns, some other jewelry, tools..."

Sarah admitted, "It makes me wonder why those were left behind."

"Us, too. But based on the past year, I'm sure you'll figure it out. :) "

Sarah smiled at the phone and then texted, "I hope so." Then she put it back into her pocket and focused on shampooing Spike.

An hour and fifteen minutes later, Spike and Whiskey were wrestling over a plush two-foot alligator with a dog's clenched jaws at each end in a game of tug-of-war when Tony walked back through the Coiffure's green door. Sarah walked toward him and stopped at the counter.

He spoke before she had the chance to say hello. "Sarah, Daphne Smith said to tell you that the thief came in through a ground-floor open window. She said you texted, but she didn't respond as she was on call. She was the potential client I was meeting with. She's concerned about her safety, and Pierre's, and that of her home."

"Oh, wow. I can understand that. French bulldogs have been targeted by thieves. Lady Gaga's three dogs are a prime example." Sarah's mouth puckered like she had sucked a bitter orange. "Tony, do you know if she has other valuables that were left behind? I've been thinking about what was taken, and it's an eclectic mix of a coin collection, a couple of pieces of jewelry while other jewelry were untouched and not taken, Daphne's coat and shoes...it doesn't make sense. And why rob so many places in one night or at one time?"

"I don't know, Sarah. Those are good questions. And yes, Daphne has a lot of very nice things that weren't stolen. And she's creeped out by the idea someone uninvited was in her space and touched her stuff."

"I would be, too," Sarah said. "I hope you can help her. So it's true, the rumors about you starting a new company and branching out from the fitness centers." Sarah smiled at him.

"It is. Some of the people working out with me have served in the military and some are ex-special forces so it seemed like a good fit.”

“Smart. And I know who to call now next time I get threats or suspicious packages,” Sarah only sort-of joked.

“Threats, yes, call us. But if you get a suspicious package, call nine-one-one or Chief James first. Don’t take any chances.” He turned toward the two dogs who were still play-fighting over the toy. “Come on, Spike. We have to get going. The camera awaits. He looks so good, Sarah. Thank you.” He ran his credit card through the reader on the counter and added a gracious tip, before bending down and adjusting the black bow tie that was askew on the pit bull’s collar. Whiskey trotted alongside them to the door and slurped Spike’s jowl before he walked out the door.

After cleaning the grooming tables, Emily swept the floors while Sarah gathered all of the towels of the day and threw them in the wash and then refilled the shampoo bottles from the gallon jugs in a cabinet. It was their daily routine and they moved about on autopilot, until the door of the Coiffure opened and George, the over sixty-five-year-old owner of Produce and More, entered holding his Chihuahua Chutney with both hands out firmly in front of him, away from his body.

Sarah smelled the rotten eggs and manure before George said a word.

“Oh my god,” Em said, moving her arm up over her nose.

“I’m so sorry, Sarah. But I didn’t know what else to do.” George’s sad brown eyes pleaded with hers. “He got out and ran straight toward the compost and fertilizer, and I swear he dove into it. The missus didn’t know what to do as she couldn’t get him out. So she called me, and I came home and found him rolling around having the time of his life." George coughed from the stench. "I know we don't have an appointment—"

Sarah cut him off, "Plop him in the far left tub." She opened the hinged counter so he could pass through.

Emily was already donning the big elbow length leather gloves they used to deal with this vicious little devil. She pulled oversized rubber gloves on top of the leather. "Okay. Ready when you are, Sarah," Em said.

Sarah covered her arms in leather and rubber as well, slid a soft muzzle onto the small dog's snout, and asked George to stand back once Emily had a hold of Chutney. Sarah turned on the hose and sprayed the dog all over, and Chutney squirmed and snarled and snapped inside the muzzle in the direction of the arms and hands that held him steady.

"I'm so sorry she behaves this way," George said, as his dog was covered in suds and scrubbed to remove all traces of smelliness he had grounded into his fur.

Sarah was glad he was peanut-sized so it didn't take long before the rinse water ran clear, and he was off for his blow out. She glanced at her phone for the time and was grateful she would still be on time to visit Mrs. Maslow.

When Chutney was warm and dry, Sarah handed him off to George and then removed the muzzle. George expressed his appreciation for the emergency session by paying double the going rate and saying, "Thank you. Thank you. Thank you so much. He smells tolerable now. I really don't know how we'd survive without you girls."

"You're welcome, George," Sarah said.

"But you may not want to let Chutney off a leash...ever." Emily grinned.

Sarah locked the door after they left. "What a day! Em, do you mind if I take the map home tonight?"

"Of course not, Sarah. And tomorrow I expect a full report on what was stolen from the antique shop."

"Absolutely." Sarah moved the towels from the washer to the dryer and she threw hers and Emily's apron in the wash. She wasn't sure if the stench from Chutney had gotten on them but she wasn't taking any chances.

"Have a good night, Em. We're gonna head out."

"You too, Sarah. See you tomorrow, Whisk." Emily patted the cattle dog's head.

CHAPTER 11

As Sarah and Whiskey walked up Main Street, Sarah swore the rotten egg and manure smell lingered around her like dust around Pigpen in the *Peanuts* comic strip. Even in the summer breeze, the scent didn't waft away. She said a silent prayer that she wouldn't too strongly assault Mrs. Maslow's nasal passages.

When they got to the park entrance, Whiskey took a few steps into the park, but Sarah called him back to her side. "Not yet, boy. We have a stop to make first."

He cocked his head to the side and eyed her suspiciously. But when he saw her in front of Bill's, he zoomed past her and up Bill's front steps.

"No, boy. We aren't visiting Bill right now." The porch was empty of the man, but the gallon jar of dog treats was atop the table. Whiskey plopped his butt next to a chair and eyed the treats. He looked pointedly at Sarah and then back at the treats.

"Oh brother. Okay. You can have one." Sarah climbed the stairs and opened the treat container. She made him give her his paw and then jump for it, working for his treat. "Now, we need to go next door." She walked down the stairs, about ten more feet on the sidewalk with Whiskey at her side, and then onto the porch of the big Victorian with the huge bay windows. She could see straight into the store and to the side windows, where she noticed that the glass had already been replaced. That was fast, Sarah thought. She opened the doors to the store and Whiskey walked ahead of her. The scent of lemon, furniture oil, and the must of old books tickled Sarah's nose, along with maybe a bit of dust or dampness.

Mrs. Maslow was in her sixties. She wore a white blouse, a midi length full, flowered skirt, and tan leather sandals. Her graying hair was cut into a wavy bob. Her face broke into a smile at the sight of Whiskey and Sarah. And she walked toward them from behind a big wooden counter that held glass casing. "So good to see you both," she said, extending her hand to Sarah. Only inches from Sarah's legs, Whiskey parked his butt on the wooden floor.

"Thank you for agreeing to talk with me, Mrs. Maslow."

"Please, Sarah, call me Glenda. And thank you again for noticing our broken window and for calling the police."

"Of course. We were helping Bill, Gladys, and Janice, as I'm sure you've heard. What happened to you and to Micas Brighton was just terrible."

"Especially dear Micas. I can't believe he's no longer with us. Who would do such a thing? He was a lovely man and so knowledgeable about antiques and art." She shook her head and rubbed her lipsticked lips together.

"Had he helped out at your store before?"

"Oh yes. The few times we've gone away the last couple of years. You know, on a buying trip or to see our daughters, Micas has been here. He said it gave him something to do, something hands on, besides all of his research and writing. He's brilliant when it comes to antiques, knowing what to buy and what has value. He's even an expert at authentication."

Sarah frowned. "You mean like being able to tell if something is a forgery?"

"Yes, that, or if a book is a first edition or what period a particular painting was done. His knowledge of Paul de Lamerie's silver work was astounding, for example. He saved us a pretty penny on a pair of candlesticks we thought were the famed silversmith's but were actually some lesser known Italian replica. I'm going to miss his brilliance." Tears filled Glenda's eyes and she wiped them away with the back of her gold ringed fingers.

"I wish I would have known him more," Sarah said. "I'm sure you were probably busy with the graduation and everything, but did you hear from him while you were gone? I mean, were there any problems here at the store?"

"No, none at all. He left us notes about Saturday's customers and the things he sold. We're closed on Sundays. But on Saturday someone had inquired about a very specific Tiffany lamp, and so he did some research and gave us some ideas where we could find it. And he added that customer's name into our book where we keep the wishlists. Nothing was out of the ordinary. At least not until the window was broken." She gave a slight shrug of her shoulders.

"I don't think I've heard what was stolen from here. I know some of the other places lost jewelry and a coin collection. What did you lose to the thief or thieves?"

"It took us a while to go through things, as you can imagine; we have quite an extensive inventory over our two floors." Glenda moved her arms around in a way that reminded Sarah of Vanna White showing off the merchandise and trips. "A couple of paintings that were in a back room have gone missing, which we told the police. We had just gotten them in and hadn't even had time to photograph them yet or officially add them to the inventory."

"Oh that's too bad," Sarah said. "What kind of paintings? What were they of and were they by someone famous?"

"We aren't sure. They looked like landscapes from Fairfield Porter but they hadn't been examined yet or authenticated. Like I said, we had just gotten them in. But they are now gone and our safe was broken into. There wasn't much in it but a bit of money and some sentimental things. And our computer was stolen from the office, along with one detachable hard drive."

Sarah squinted her eyes in thought. "Was it a laptop or desktop?"

"Laptop. They took the computer but left the mouse and cords."

"And how did they get into the safe?"

"They pried it from the wall and cut it open."

Sarah's eyes grew in astonishment. "But that's so noisy. You'd think someone would have heard."

"Yes, but you could say the same about the breaking of the window."

"Yes, of course. I'm so sorry you were robbed. Was the laptop backed up to the cloud?"

"Most of it. The police have alerted pawn shops, they said. And we have alerted our fellow antique dealers about the paintings though we couldn't do much but describe them."

"Well, I hope you get the computer back and the paintings and anything else that was stolen."

"Thank you, Sarah. We know you've helped the police solve mysteries, so if you have any ideas about this or any more questions, we'd be happy to talk with you again."

"Thank you. Oh, I do have one more question. Do you have a security system for your store? I didn't hear an alarm or anything going off when we found the screen removed and the broken glass."

"No, we don't. We've never needed one. This has been such a safe town, and we've lived here for much of our lives."

"So no cameras or anything either?"

Glenda shook her head no. "Never even considered it."

"I can understand. I appreciate your time. I'm sorry you had to come home and deal with this after a joyous weekend. Come on, Whiskey, we should head home."

The dog stood, took two steps toward Glenda, and then rubbed against her leg like he was trying to make her feel better, before he turned and walked to the door.

"He's a good dog," Glenda said.

"He really is," Sarah agreed. "Thank you again for your time. Enjoy your evening."

This time they passed Bill's house without stopping and cut through the park that was only sparsely populated since it was many people's dinner hour. Whiskey kept his sniffing of canine personal ads to a minimum, which signaled to Sarah that he was hungry and determined to get home.

As Whiskey and Sarah came through the front door of their craftsman bungalow, Jared was walking through the open back door, carrying a platter of grilled chicken breasts and the barbecue tongs. "Hello, mi'lady," he greeted.

"Good day, good sir." Sarah curtsied while holding an imaginary skirt out on both sides of her jeans. "That food smells incredible."

"A simple and colorful meal tonight: grilled chicken brushed with barbecue sauce and grilled peppers, purple onions, zucchini, and yellow squash. And it is ready now so you'll need to wait on your shower."

"Okay. I'll grab plates and set the table."

"I already did," Jared said, leaning toward her and kissing her cheek. "You could feed Whiskey."

"On it," Sarah said, heading into the kitchen and getting the dog's food from the freezer. She nuked a serving of the raw dog food in the microwave to soften and warm it and then put the bowl on the floor. Whiskey inhaled it before Sarah had finished washing her hands. "Jeez, dog. Did you even taste it?"

He looked up at her, his amber eyes pleading, and hit his empty bowl with his paw to signal he wanted more.

"Sorry, bud. No seconds. But I can give you a rawhide chew." Sarah reached into the glass container of dog treats that sat on the kitchen counter and pulled one out. Whiskey took off with it to his bed in the living room.

Once Sarah was seated across from Jared in the dining room and they had food on their plates, she asked, "How was your day?"

"Good. Lots of business today. And lots of gossip about the shooting of Micas Brighton."

Sarah swallowed a bite of chicken. "Anything interesting?"

Jared looked directly into Sarah's eyes and said, "Would you call an execution-style killing interesting?"

Sarah's fork fell from her hand and clanged on her plate. "WHAT?!?"

"I overheard Barb and Trish talking about it. Trish is worried the mob is moving into town." Jared frowned. "If the mob killed a historian, it had to be that he was working for them in some capacity. It wouldn't be random." He shook his head. "None of it makes sense."

"So, execution-style means a shot to the back of the head, right?"

Jared nodded. "At close range and often the person being shot is kneeling or restrained."

"Why would someone kill Micas Brighton that way? Do you think it was to make a statement or give a warning?" Sarah pushed her plate a few inches from her. Her appetite had vanished like smoke in the wind.

"I don't know. Oh, but they did say one more thing. The gun was at the scene, but it had been wiped clean."

Sarah's mouth opened in astonishment. "Let me get this right. So someone enters Micas Brighton's house, maybe restrains him, shoots him at close range or maybe even point-blank in the head, and then leaves the gun behind at the scene and it has no prints. I'm guessing it probably isn't registered to anyone either."

"I didn't hear anyone mention that, but logic would dictate that is probably the case."

"And it all happened right here in Cottageville as opposed to New York or Miami, or even Kansas City."

"You really should eat some more food, Sarah. Your brain needs nutrition to process all of the clues."

"And did anyone say whether or not the break-ins and the murder are tied to each other? Was the gun left at the scene the one that had been stolen on Saturday during the concert?"

Jared stabbed an arc of onion and placed it into his mouth. He chewed thoughtfully before saying, "No, they didn't. But no one in the cafe today acted like they were afraid a killer was on the loose or that the shooting was random. No word on whether the gun was the one stolen."

"Yeah, well, when the killer leaves the weapon at the scene, it seems unlikely..." Sarah's voice trailed off. "I have some news, too." She filled him in on the map, the texts with Daphne and Rebecca Davis, as well as her visit with Glenda Maslow.

Jared finished the last few bites of food on his plate and then said, "So the thieves had time to crowbar and crack or drill or whatever a safe? And they stole electronic records and two paintings? Did she tell you what was in the safe?"

"Not really. But I wonder if the thief or thieves were the same at all of the places. I mean, why would you take a laptop one place but ignore the laptops at the others? Or why take one or pieces of jewelry when there are more in the same box? It's so strange." Sarah ate a few pieces of zucchini and a bite of chicken. The barbecue sauce was tangy and sweet, just like she preferred it.

"It is. You know when we've figured out a robbery before, there was a clear motive for what was taken. But this seems random or like things were taken just to prove they could be."

"Do you mean like trophies?"

"Kind of. I read an article once of a guy about my age who broke into cars, either ones left unlocked or ones with locks he could open, and the only things he took were owner's manuals from people's glove boxes. He left phones, change, anything else he found, and he often left one of the doors slightly ajar so the message was 'Hey, you've been robbed'."

"So it was like a sport to him? But instead of mounted deer heads and taxidermied ducks, he collected owner's manuals?" Sarah's eyebrows were arched in question.

"Exactly. Maybe it's something like that."

"Do you know what kind of gun was used on Micas?"

"I don't. You could ask one of our law enforcement friends."

"I could, but I'm not sure the information has been made public, officially." Sarah eyed Jared and bit her bottom lip in thought.

"That's true. But in the past they have been surprisingly free flowing with information with you."

"Yeah, well, I've also found myself in the middle of things...for better or worse." Sarah flashed Jared a sheepish smile.

"True. At least this time all you discovered was a broken window. I'll take that over hate mail or finding someone victimized any day."

Sarah managed to eat more than half of her dinner. "This was really good, but I'm going to save the rest. The idea of a possible mob hit has my stomach churning. The things I know about organized crime come from movies. Mobsters are involved in gambling, money laundering, prostitution, maybe drugs or gun-running, and their shootings are sometimes over turf wars. None of that connects easily to a retired historian in our sleepy little town in Iowa."

"There are plenty of things we don't know though. How much did you find out about Micas Brighton in your research last night?"

"Mostly work-related stuff. The papers he authored, his areas of expertise, that kind of stuff. He seemed very well respected in his field and knew a lot about sculptors and painters as well as how to date artifacts and art."

"Anything about his personal life?"

Sarah shook her head. "But I only made it through the first two or three pages of the search. The man was a prolific journal article writer."

"So maybe we start there. We look for connections. I can help you search. Let's put the food away and clean up the kitchen and then we can sit in here and use our computers and put our heads together to create a profile of who Micas Brighton was, both before he moved to Cottageville and while he was here."

"That sounds like a plan." Sarah stood and gathered Jared's and her plate and utensils and carried them into the kitchen. As she scraped her food into a glass container with a locking lid, she said to Jared, "I'm gonna jump in the shower before we do the search. I can't believe you can't smell me." Then she told him about Chutney's emergency visit and the other dogs and humans she saw throughout the day.

Jared leaned closer and audibly sniffed her hair and her shoulder like he would the nose of a glass of fine wine. "You don't smell sulfuric or like manure. You have that Sarah scent that I love."

"You're a master at wooing women." Sarah kissed him.

When they broke apart he said, "No women. Only you."

"Smooth talker." She stole another quick kiss before padding off to the bathroom for that shower.

Five minutes later, she was dressed in dog print sleep shorts and a cattle dog tank top and back at the dining table where Jared had set up both of their computers on one side of the table. He had placed two legal pads and pens next to the laptops and he was squinting at his screen. "I've started a list of the places where Micas worked, and I assumed lived, before he came here. He studied art history at Yale and Harvard and then spent some time at Oxford and in London. He worked in D.C. as a consultant to national museums while teaching at Georgetown. Then it looks like he was at the University of Chicago and then back to the Boston area before going to New York and consulting with Sotheby's, Christie's, and Bonhams."

"I know Sotheby's and Christie's, but I'm unfamiliar with Bonhams."

"I had only known the name so I looked them up. Oldest auction house in the world, but smaller than the other two. Privately owned. Based in London. Handles art, antiquities, jewelry, classic and vintage cars, arms and armor, and wine.”

“That’s quite an eclectic mix.”

“Eh, basically anything that could be priceless and collected.”

The synapses in Sarah’s skull felt like exploding pyrotechnics. “The things that were stolen fit those categories, right? Daphne’s couture, paintings, jewelry—though I doubt it was expensive, the coin collection...and I still don’t know what else was taken from those two other houses.”

“Yes, I agree that those things fit categories. But the thief or thieves of random stuff isn’t taking them to auction. Most likely they’ll show up at a pawn shop or on eBay. Think about it, Sarah, why do people break into houses and steal?”

Sarah started naming reasons and checked them off one hand by touching her pointer finger from her right hand to her thumb, followed by the four fingers, on her right hand as she said, “Money for drugs, professional thief, revenge, impulsive, addicted to the thrill of stealing?” On the last one she raised her eyebrows.

“I would add needing whatever was taken due to poverty or whatever. I’m thinking of Hugo’s story of *Les Misérables*. Jean, the main character, stole because he was hungry. There is all kinds of hunger and many of the reasons on your list speak to that.”

“Wise like Yoda.” Sarah squeezed his bicep. “Do you think we should work on the assumption that the thief was the same in all of the break-ins or do you think it was multiple people together or like an orchestrated ring of thieves that all struck at once?” Sarah pulled the map from her backpack and placed it between their laptops. She examined the Sharpie marks that signified the locations. “These ones—" she moved her right pointer finger in a circle over Main Street, "would take someone a ten-minute walk from the antique store to the Davis' house."

"Yes, if they didn't stop at two places in between, but they did."

Sarah unconsciously rubbed the point of her chin while staring at the map. "Hey, didn't John say there were drops of blood in the antique store, like on the floor and going up the stairs?"

Jared looked up and to the right like the answer might be written on the dining room ceiling. "I think so."

"Well, no one I talked to mentioned blood in their house. I wonder if there wasn't any or if it just wasn't mentioned. I never thought to ask about it."

"If no one's house had blood, that could be for a number of reasons."

"I know. One, the antique store could have been robbed after the other places. Two, more than one thief or thieves hit the places. Three, the bleeding could have stopped, or maybe if the thief drove, a first aid kit was in the car."

Jared jumped in with, "Or four, the antique store just happened to be robbed on the same night that someone decided to steal things from a few houses. Think about it, Sarah, we have no proof the robberies are connected. Whoever burgled the houses went through windows or doors. Isn't that what you said you found out?"

Sarah's eyes bugged like a pug's. "And someone wanted or needed to get into the antique store bad enough that they were willing to remove a screen and break a window. They also took a chance with the noise of power tools on the safe. That seems like a different M.O."

She rubbed her hands together. "I feel like we are finally getting somewhere." But then her face fell. "But I still have no idea what it means."

Jared chuckled and put his arm around her and pulled her to his side. "It's still early and we are still lacking in clues. But I'm sure we will figure it out. Keep asking questions and we'll keep researching Micas Brighton's life. Somewhere, the answers are out there." He raised his arms up over his head and stretched. "But I need to call it a night. Three-thirty comes too early."

CHAPTER 12

The next morning, clad in faded jeans and a "my cattle dog would side eye you so hard" gray t-shirt and carrying her empty coffee tumbler, Sarah followed Whiskey on his sniff-fest through Cottageville Park. She spied John Beams trailing an on-leash Coco Chanel by the empty swing set. "Morning, John," Sarah called.

He looked over his shoulder toward her. "Hey, Sarah."

"You on dog duty this a.m.?"

Whiskey sniffed his friend's ear and then he circled around behind her and sniffed her butt. She jumped around so they were face to face. Sarah and John chuckled.

"Braid went on a business trip, so it's me and Ms. Chanel for the rest of the week."

"At least she's not needy."

"Yes. I'm glad for that, and I'm off today so we'll have plenty of time together."

"Hey, may I ask you something about the robberies?"

John flashed her a grin. "You can ask, but I can't guarantee I'll answer."

"Fair enough. Em and I plotted the places burgled on a map. It's almost a straight line except for Daphne's. I remember you saying something about blood in the antique shop."

"Yes," John said, as Coco Chanel flattened herself on the ground in submissive mode to Whiskey.

"Stand your ground, girl," Sarah said. "You're his equal, at least." Then she turned her attention back to John. "Anyway, how much blood was there and where was it?"

"Not a ton but a definite trail from the window through the store and up the stairs."

"Was there blood by the wall safe and on the desk?"

John's lips flattened into a line and he squinted his eyes at her. "Sarah, how do you know about those things? We kept them out of the press and told the Maslows not to feed the gossip mill."

"Mrs. Maslow told me," Sarah quietly admitted. "In her defense, I think it was because she knows I received Citizen of the Year for helping solve those other cases."

"Everyone in town knows that, Sarah. And we've appreciated your help. But please don't tell anyone about what was taken from the antique store."

"Uhh, in full disclosure, I've already talked to Jared."

"He's to claim partner confidentiality. Please tell me you've told no one else."

"I haven't," Sarah confirmed. "But why the secrecy?"

John stared at her for a couple of beats. His expression was blank, but Sarah felt sure he was thinking, debating what he could say and what needed to be held back. She waited, but when he didn't respond, she asked, "About the blood, was any found at the houses that were robbed?"

"No. No blood."

That confirmed at least one of Sarah's suspicions, but then something else occurred to her. "Did the trail of blood come out the front door of the antique store? We were on the front porch waiting for you, but I didn't think to look down for droplets of blood."

John released an audible sigh. "Yes, Sarah. Blood was on the porch, and before you ask, it went down the couple of steps and onto the sidewalk."

Sarah opened her mouth to ask one more question, but John continued, "And there it stopped. No trail extended down the sidewalk."

Sarah's eyes widened as if they could catch the truth before it disappeared. In her mind's eye, she saw the blood trail stop at the curb. "Because the thief got into a car." Her voice was quiet, steady, almost reverent.

"That's what we think, but you are to tell no one. Got it?"

"Absolutely."

Both dogs were now lying on the ground side by side waiting for their humans to get on with the walk.

Sarah was just about to say goodbye to John and urge Whiskey onward when another question popped into her head. "I heard Micas Brighton was shot execution style and the gun was left at the scene. What kind of gun was it?"

"Oh for the love of God, who told you all of that?"

Sarah had never heard John sound so exasperated. "Uh, Mrs. Chief and the mayor were overheard at Java and Juice." Sarah's stomach clenched. She hated to rat them out.

John ran a hand through his curly black hair. His eyes had turned dark. "A 9 mm Glock. Clean of prints."

"Serial numbers?" Sarah asked. She remembered reading somewhere at some point that some guns had numbers in multiple places.

"The one on the frame was filed off. The slide and barrel I'm unsure of. The techs will take it apart during processing."

"Hmm. I hope that provides some kind of lead."

"We do, too. And Sarah, I know how much you enjoy solving mysteries, and we really do appreciate how much you've helped us in the past. But as your friend, I have to warn you. This thing with Micas has all of the markings of a professional hit. Don't risk your life by sticking your nose into it. I don't want you to get hurt or to wind up dead."

"Me either. Thank you for the warning, John. I'll stick to the house break-ins." She grinned at him showing her teeth, and unlike a monkey with the same grin, she meant hers to be teasing and friendly.

"Good plan...if you must solve something." The last part was mumbled. "Come on, princess, let's get your business done and go home. I'm sure Sarah and Whiskey don't want to be late for work." He gave a quick tug on Coco Chanel's leather leash to get her to stand and walk with him.

"He's right, Whisk. Let's go say hi to Bill, then stop by Java and Juice, and get to work. We have a busy day of grooming ahead. Or well, I do. You have a busy day of greeting, playing, and napping." He looked up at her and stretched his black lips into a smile before speed-walking up the path toward Main Street. Sarah chased after his red and white-tipped tail.

Fewer than twenty minutes later, they were at the Coiffure saying hello to Emily, whose hair was now temporarily dyed red, white, and blue and was plaited into two braids. She wore a white smocked sundress and her black Doc Marten boots under a British tan canvas apron.

"Oh my," Sarah said when she saw Em's hair. "Whether you're being festive or ironic, you're totally rocking the look."

Em grinned wider than a Cheshire cat. "Thank you. And you've got on a new shirt."

"I do and thank you for noticing. I saw it on Etsy and couldn't resist."

"Somebody sure knows their cattle dogs. So, what's for breakfast and lunch today?"

"Peach and pecan scones with a caramel drizzle and ahi tuna, avocado, and cucumber salad. It may have too many onions in it for you, but they'll be easy enough to pick out."

"Both sound yummy. I don't mind the onions. I just don't like to have dragon breath." Emily smirked.

"No one wants to have dragon breath...except maybe a dragon." Sarah handed Emily a wax paper wrapped scone. "Jared said they were wrapping these to go because with the drizzle they might be sticky."

"Fortunately for us, we have a lot of sinks." One side of Em's mouth rose in a half-smile and she winked.

"You're on a roll today." Sarah broke off a bit of scone and popped it into her mouth before she went to the apron rack and grabbed the apron that matched Emily's. Then she walked to the dryer and pulled out the things left in it yesterday. She folded and stacked the towels above the wash stations and hung the two dog print aprons that they wore and then washed after Chutney's visit.

Sarah and Emily ate their scones while they discussed a game plan for today's clients as it was a day of grooming all bigger dogs. First to arrive would be Katie Smith, who was supermodel thin and had long, shiny black hair, and was dog-mom to two snow-white samoyeds named Babs and Tabs. The dogs weren't tall or huge, but they were blessed with thick, fluffy double coats of fur. Sarah estimated Babs and Tabs to weigh around fifty pounds each, about the same weight as Whiskey. But because of their fur, she allocated an extra thirty minutes for them in the schedule. Then, right before lunch, harlequin Great Dane Lilly, a one hundred and twenty pound beauty that always left Whiskey bumbling around her like a lovestruck pre-pubescent boy, would be arriving. Her human companions, Lisa and Holly, owned the Whispering Pines Boutique B&B, Cottageville's only inn and more recently, its most celebrated and sought-after wedding venue. And the two dogs that would round out their active afternoon included a one hundred and thirty pound black Russian terrier named Onyx and a one hundred and twenty pound Great Pyrenees named Pedro. Sarah and Emily would work together on the last three dogs as none of them could be efficiently bathed, dried, and groomed by only two hands.

"Remind me again why we agreed to book all of these dogs on the same day?" Emily ran a hand over her face. "Last time we did this, my muscles screamed at me."

"What did they scream? Hey, stupid?" Sarah quipped.

"Something like that. But with more cuss words." Emily giggled.

"So you had dirty words from your deltoids and swearing from your soleus?"

"Very funny. Remind me again where my soleus is. I don't want to Google."

Sarah chuckled. "Your calf."

"Yes, there. And my back and abs and arms and neck. Every muscle in my body screamed. I felt like I spent hours at Big T's."

"Except it was man's best friend fitness." Sarah ate the last bite of her scone and washed it down with a swig of black dark roast coffee.

The green door of Coiffure opened and Whiskey ran to greet the day's first clients, while Sarah said hi to Katie Smith, who was wearing a well-cut black pants suit over white silk t-shirt and who she realized had cut her gorgeous raven hair to shoulder level. "You cut your hair," Sarah stated the obvious.

"I did. Sergio insisted I needed a fresh summer look." Katie had wispy bangs touching her forehead like butterfly wings and a precision cut across the back that was so sharp it could have been measured with a ruler. The sleek curve of it hugged her neck like it had been sculpted, not snipped, and the shine in her hair caught the light like ink still wet on paper. Sarah reached out before she could stop herself, fingers hovering just above Katie's shoulder. "It looks amazing," she said, though something in her chest twisted—admiration, maybe, or something more complicated. It was the first time since she moved to Cottageville that Sarah thought that maybe, just maybe, Sergio's exorbitant prices were worth it. What kind of vision could he create for her Irish-red locks that spent most of their life wrapped up with an elastic that her hairdresser Jackie—though competent but not an *artiste*—couldn't see?

"I'm still getting used to it," Katie admitted. "He chopped it off yesterday late afternoon. And I'm pretty sure, I lost a whole pound." Her smile beamed her light from within.

"That's one way to lose weight...not that you need it," Sarah said.

Emily grabbed Babs' leash and guided the dog into the grooming area. Sarah took the other leash from Katie and said, "Can you give us two and a half to three hours?"

"Yes, but could I actually pick them up after lunch? I have a meeting in Cedar Rapids this morning."

"Absolutely. We can keep them as long as you need. It's not a problem."

"Bless you," Katie said.

Once they were alone again and Babs and Tabs were in side by side tubs, Emily asked, "What did Mrs. Maslow say?"

"She was grateful I noticed the broken window and called the police. She thanked me multiple times."

"Yeah, but what was stolen?" Emily worked her sudsy fingers into Bab's luxurious fur.

"Only a few things, a couple paintings and their laptop." Sarah kept her promise to John by not mentioning the safe.

"Did you find out anything else?"

"Not really. Jared and I did some online sleuthing to piece together some of the places Micas Brighton lived before he came here. He's lived and worked a lot of places in the U.S. and he lived in at least two places in England."

"I wonder what brought him to Cottageville," Emily mused aloud.

"Nothing answered that." While Sarah worked the shampoo into Tabs, giving the dog a massage from head to tail, she wondered who in town may have interacted with Micas regularly. The closest research university was more than thirty miles away. Janice Jenkins was likely the most well-traveled person in Cottageville—a true citizen of the world who spoke at least five languages, setting her apart from most in the small town. But Sarah hadn't asked her if she knew Micas Brighton. She made a mental note to do so this evening...before John's warning not to investigate something that may be a professional hit popped into her head. She frowned down at the dog she was washing without really seeing her.

"Whatcha thinking, Sarah?" Emily broke through her fog.

"Just wondering who was friends with Micas Brighton. Someone around here must know more than we do considering we barely met the guy."

"What about Carole at the library?" Emily offered.

Sarah's head felt like it cleared. "That's a brilliant suggestion." Carole Binds was the head librarian at the Cottageville Public Library. She was middle aged and loved bright colors and funky shaped glasses, and she was a living, walking, breathing encyclopedia of all things literature and all things Cottageville. And since the library was one of the hubs of the community—it offered computers and classes for all ages, and all kinds of programs in addition to the borrowing of books, magazines, videos, ebooks, and so much more—it was the place most citizens went at least occasionally. Plus, Carole could get almost anything for any research through an interlibrary loan.

"I should go see Carole," Sarah said, as she started the rinse water and swished Tabs' fur with her hands.

"Not today, you shouldn't," Em said. "You're not leaving me here when we have more than four hundred pounds of dog on its way."

Sarah flashed Em a look of innocence and said, "Who, me? I was just thinking out loud."

Emily raised an eyebrow. "Thinking out loud is how you end up halfway across town with a notepad and no backup."

Sarah laughed, rinsing the last of the suds from Tabs' tail. "Fine, I'll wait until the drool squad clears out. But tomorrow, I'm heading to the library."

"Tell Carole I still want that mystery book with the skeleton on the cover. She'll know the one."

"Of course she will," Sarah said. "Carole knows everything."

And this time, Sarah hoped that included whatever secrets Micas Brighton had left behind.

CHAPTER 13

At seven-forty-five the next morning, Sarah pulled open Java and Juice's red door and held it for Whiskey, who trotted straight up the counter since no one was in line. Mayor Trish and Barbara were not at their usual table. In fact, the cafe was emptier than it often was at this time of the day, but Sarah knew that plenty of people used the week before or after Independence Day for their vacations. At a table closest to the rest rooms and facing toward the front door and windows was a familiar face. Glenda Maslow waved at Sarah and then motioned for her to come near. She wore a shirtwaist dress in a white and red print and had royal blue beads around her neck.

"Good morning, Glenda. How are you today?" Sarah recognized the man across from Mrs. Maslow as her husband, but she didn't recognize the younger woman who sat to his right. That woman seemed to be about Sarah's age of twenty-eight and had sleek chestnut hair with golden highlights, vivid blue eyes, and wore a t-shirt with a couture brand logo, what were clearly designer jeans, and high heeled sandals.

"We're fine, Sarah. Do you know my husband, Peter?" She held out her hand, palm up, toward him.

"I know of him but we haven't met." Sarah stretched out her hand for him to shake. "Sarah Carter, and that red rascal over at the counter is my cattle dog Whiskey."

"Ah, the infamous duo," Peter chuckled. He had a salt and pepper goatee, a salt and pepper unibrow that reminded Sarah of a furry caterpillar, and a bit of a gut protruding against the buttons of his oxford shirt. Sarah pegged him at his mid to late sixties. To the woman next to him, he explained, "Sarah and Whiskey were honored by the mayor for their sleuthing skills even though she's a dog groomer."

Sarah smiled and shrugged her shoulders. Then she reached out her hand to the woman. "Sarah Carter, I don't believe we've met."

The woman's hand felt warm and bony but solid in hers. "Carlotta Brighton, but most people call me Lottie."

An *ohhh* sounded inside Sarah's skull, and she took a guess with her next words. "I'm sorry for your loss."

"Thank you. My father's death has been quite a shock."

"I can imagine." Sarah looked into the woman's eyes, wanting to portray her empathy.

Glenda explained, "Lottie arrived last night. She's staying at the inn."

Lottie looked down at the sundried tomato, feta, and herb omelet on her plate as Glenda's eyes tried to convey something to Sarah, but since Sarah didn't really know Glenda, she was at a loss. Instead she said, "Lottie, I know this may seem like a weird offer, but we are a small town where everyone mostly knows everyone or at least of everyone. What I mean is, if you need help with your dad's stuff or anything at all, just let me know. I can round up some friends." She pointed to the counter where Whiskey was still engaged with Jared. "That's my boyfriend. The owner of this cafe is my best friend. Her fiance owns the local hardware store. You see what I mean. We can help in any way. You don't have to do anything alone if you don't want to."

When Lottie's eyes met Sarah's they were awash with unshed tears. "That's the kindest thing anyone has ever offered. I appreciate it. I'm at...what's it called...Whispering Pines...because I couldn't bear to go into the house...where it happened."

Peter bulldozed his way into the conversation with, "The police wouldn't let you anyway. They haven't released the scene."

"Peter," Glenda hissed.

"What?" he snapped. "It's true."

Tears streamed down Lottie's face. Sarah had the urge to hug her, even though the woman looked too put together to be a hugger. "Be right back," she said, and she rushed to the counter, saying, "Paper. Pen," to Jared.

When Sarah returned to the table, she slid the piece of paper with her number on it to Lottie. "Call me anytime. Also, my business is two blocks south and one block west on Rosewood Avenue. Carter's Canine Coiffure. On the left next to the Italian restaurant. You can't miss it."

Lottie gave her a weak smile and wiped her eyes with her fingers. "Thank you, Sarah. You're so sweet."

"Well, I should let you get back to your breakfast. I need to grab mine and be on my way. But really, anything I can do to help. Just call. Or if you don't need help but want company. Jared makes amazing food and we are always open to making new friends." Sarah gave Lottie her warmest smile. "Bye, Glenda. Nice to meet you, Peter."

She returned to the counter and leaned across it to plant a kiss on Jared's lips. He filled her to-go tumbler and handed her a bag of food he had already prepared. "Wild salmon and dill salad, same scones as yesterday."

"Ooo, those were addictive."

"It's peach season so it's hard to get anything better. Do you plan to be home at the usual time? And do you mind cooking tonight or bringing take-out home with you? I need to spend a good four hours this afternoon on the plan for the Czech gallery."

"I'm on it. Go. Work. Do you. Be fabulous." Sarah grinned at him. "I love you."

At that moment Ginger, her blonde hair in a high ponytail and wearing a hot pink t-shirt under washed-so-often-they-are-almost-white denim overalls, came through the swinging doors of the back room. "I love you, too," she said to Sarah before she guffawed at her timing.

"Hey, bestie. We need some girl time."

"We're having it. On July fourth."

"Uhh, sure. And including Daniel's mother."

Sarah side-eyed the table by the rest room and saw that they were back in a conversation. So she leaned across the counter and whispered to Ginger, "That's Lottie, Micas Brighton's daughter. If she's still here on Monday, can I bring her to your house?"

"New friend?" Ginger smiled mischievously.

"Working on it."

"That's my BFF. Of course."

"Thank you." Sarah air kissed in Ginger's vicinity. "I hope Em's opened the Coiffure as now I'm running late. Love you both," she reiterated. "Come on, Whiskey. Let's go."

Emily had indeed opened the Coiffure, and she was elbows deep in the tub, washing a dog Sarah couldn't see. Whiskey raced to greet her and slurped her bare leg as she was wearing a knit black minidress under her apron.

"Who is in the tub?" Sarah asked, setting the scones on to the table and then placing the salads in the refrigerator. She took a sip of her coffee before slipping the half arc of the apron over her head.

"Tiny. You just missed Rosa." Rosa Torres had clear olive skin that Sarah envied. She had long dark hair with a bit of wave and resembled a Disney princess. The woman was forty and looked twenty and she doted on her toy poodle like it was a baby...but it was full-grown at four pounds, Tiny was more like a preemie. Sarah wondered how anyone cohabited with such a small dog without accidentally stepping on it.

When she looked in the tub, Tiny looked like the proverbial

drowned rat. He was shivering, despite the warmth of the water. "It's okay, bud. You're almost through." Sarah scratched the top of his wet head.

To Em, she said, "I met Micas Brighton's daughter this morning in Java and Juice. That's why I was late." Sarah went on to describe Lottie and mentioned her offer to help Lottie go through her dad's things or clear out the house or whatever, when it was time.

"I'll help and I'm sure I could get Travis and Taylor to do so, too, if it isn't a work day for them."

"That's nice of you. We'll see if she calls."

"Does she have siblings?" Em rinsed the dog until the water ran clear and on such a small dog, it only took a minute.

"She didn't say. I officially met Peter Maslow, too."

Em nodded her head once signalling she heard Sarah. She held a towel in both hands and used it to scoop up the shivering dog and then swaddled Tiny against her chest. The little poodle suddenly stilled. "That's it, baby. You're safe."

"How are your muscles today?" Sarah asked.

"Happy to groom such a sweet little dog."

"Drake Farmer should be here any minute with Annabelle. I'll take her while you finish Tiny and eat your breakfast." Annabelle was a sable coated akita that stood a couple of inches taller than Whiskey. She was a sweet girl who loved to play, but her favorite thing to do was to hang her head out of her human's 5 series BMW sedan and let her tongue flap in the breeze.

And just as Sarah was thinking that, the black car pulled to the curb with the dog's head poking out of the passenger window. "Here she is," Sarah said, as Whiskey slid across the floor into the door.

Drake pushed open the door as Sarah yelled, "Just a minute." She helped Whiskey to stand and move out of the way, before she opened the door widely. Annabelle trotted inside and she and Whiskey started the sniffing dance steps.

"Morning, Drake," Sarah said. His mirrored sunglasses hid his brown eyes. He was dressed in jeans and army green t-shirt that stretched across his mocha skin and muscles. "Anything I should know about? Itching? Too much shedding?"

"No. She's good, just needs the usual."

"Okay. Give us two hours then."

"Thanks, Sarah." He left and Sarah said, "Come on, girl, follow me. Whiskey, let's get her into the walk-in tub."

Three and a half hours later, they had a bit of a lull after lunch, with twenty minutes until their next client and fifty minutes until the client after that. Sarah eyed Emily who was playing with her phone, but Em looked up and caught her eye. "You want to go to the library?" She raised one eyebrow.

"I do," Sarah admitted.

"Have at it then. I got things covered here. I don't need help with the affenpinscher."

"Okay. I'll be quick about it. I promise." Sarah pulled her apron over her head and then left it on the table. "Whiskey, you stay here with Em."

He sighed and curled into a ball on the floor near the table.

Cottageville Public Library was on Main Street one block from Sarah's street. At the end of last year, Jared had been painting a Christmas scene on the big plate glass windows on the library when an out of control semi truck crashed into his ladder and the building, causing glass to fly, the steel framing of the building to bend, and Jared to end up in the ER. He was lucky to break his leg and that he didn't lose his life.

In the months since, the library had raised money to repair and rebuild, and the new side of the library looked exactly like the old. Sarah had been amazed at how the community members had stepped up and donated money and time to make that a reality.

When she entered the library through the big glass sliding doors, Sarah felt assaulted by the air conditioning. It probably wasn't set very cold or on full blast, but compared to the heat and bit of humidity outside, she felt the contrast. A woman with russett corkscrew curls, a flowered dress, and a big smile was manning the front desk. Sarah had seen her around town, knew she was new—as in hired post-Jared's accident—and thought her name was Chelsea, but they had never met.

Sarah approached the desk and gave the woman, whom she guessed to be in her early forties, her friendliest smile. "Hi. I'm Sarah Carter, and I'm here to see Carole Binds."

"Hi, Sarah. I'm Chelsea King, assistant librarian. Carole is at lunch with the board. It's their monthly meeting. Is there anything I can help you with?"

"Oh, no, thank you. Will Carole be back later this afternoon?"

"She will, but she'll be handling the end of the month paperwork. Would you like to make an appointment to see her tomorrow or some other time this week?"

"No. I'll just stop back at another time. Please tell her Sarah stopped by though. She has my number.”

Disappointed, Sarah turned to leave and then remembered her manners. She spun back around. “It was lovely to meet you, Chelsea. Welcome to Cottageville.”

In five minutes, Sarah was back inside the Coiffure with Whiskey and Em.

“That was quick,” Emily said.

“She wasn’t there. But I met the new assistant librarian. She seems nice.”

“The message board is quiet today. No more speculation on the robberies. Nothing about Micas Brighton.”

“Maybe the chatterers are on vacation.”

“I kind of wish I was,” Emily admitted.

“Oh, yeah. Where do you want to go?”

“Anywhere really. I’ve spent my whole life here. We went to Disneyland once when I was a kid. But I don’t remember much, except there’s a photo of me as maybe a four or five year old hugging the leg of Goofy and his big white glove was on my shoulder, holding me close.”

“Goofy makes sense or maybe Pluto, since you love dogs. You’ve never struck me as a Disney princess kind of person.” Sarah grinned at her assistant.

“Yeah, give me Wonder Woman or Iron Man any day. No floofy women in distress.” Emily stamped one combat booted foot on the floor, which caused Whiskey to give her the eye until the door opened and Sam the affenpinscher entered the Coiffure, walking in front of his affable human Helen Goode, who was Sarah’s residential mail carrier. “Hey, Sarah. On my lunch break so I’m making this quick.

Can I come back and get him around five?"

"Yes, I'll be here until five-fifteen or five-thirty at the latest."

"Sounds good. I shouldn't be later than five. Be good, little one." With that she scurried out the door.

"You still want this one, Em?"

"Who is coming next?"

"Charlie the Chinook."

"What a sweetheart but too big. I'll take Sam. You wash Charlie, and I'll take whoever comes after that."

"Sounds like a plan." Sarah handed Sam to Emily, who placed him in a stainless steel tub while she cooed at him, "Who's a handsome boy? Who's a handsome boy? You are, Sam. Yes, you are." His beady black eyes in his shiny black fur reflected her affection.

Sarah used the short break in the schedule to go online and order two strombolis and an antipasti platter from the Italian-American restaurant next door for pick up at five-fifteen. *There*, she thought, *I've handled dinner*. She smiled to herself and awaited Charlie's arrival.

CHAPTER 14

After they finished dinner and Jared had returned to his studio to do more work, Sarah's phone rang with an unknown number. "Hello?" she answered, her voice tentative.

"Sarah? It's Lottie Brighton. I know you said I could call and I wasn't sure I would, but then your boyfriend assured me that you were serious about your offer. I talked to him before the Maslows and I left Java and Juice."

Over the stromboli, Jared had mentioned he had reiterated to Lottie that they and their friends would help with her dad's house or anything else she needed. He had even asked if she wanted to join them for dinner on Saturday, but she said she didn't know her plans yet. She was taking everything one day at a time, awaiting the police's release of her dad's body and getting the all-clear to enter the house.

"Hi, Lottie. Yes, I was serious." Sarah let the comment hang to see where Lottie would take the conversation.

"I was wondering if you'd like to come to Whispering Pines for breakfast tomorrow. I checked with the women who run this place and they said that would be okay."

"I can, but it would need to be early since I need to be at work by eight, eight-fifteen at the latest." Sarah made a mental note to text Em when she got off the phone.

"They start serving at six-thirty. Is that too early for you? I'm still on West Coast time."

"That would be perfect. Thank you for the invitation."

"Do you know where it is?" Lottie's voice sounded stronger, more assured than when Sarah first answered the phone.

"Yes. Small town and all of that." Sarah smiled even though Lottie couldn't see her face.

"Oh, right. Okay then. I'll see you at six-thirty."

"Sounds good." And just as Sarah was about to disconnect she heard Lottie say, "Oh wait. They said your dog...what's his name? Some kind of alcohol...can come, too."

"Whiskey. And thank you. See you tomorrow morning."

Sarah texted Emily asking if she could open tomorrow just in case Whiskey and she were running late. And then she wondered how much gas was in her old CJ. She didn't drive much, preferring to walk, but Whispering Pines was on the outskirts of town and too far to walk, especially on the tight time schedule she had tomorrow.

And since she'd have to get up extra early and get Whiskey walked beforehand, Sarah went into the bedroom to pick out her clothes. Usually she wore one of her many dog t-shirts and jeans for work, but since she was meeting Lottie at Whispering Pines, which was architecturally stunning with a curved staircase, plush carpets, and clustered upholstered seating areas, she decided to forgo her everyday clothes in favor of an evergreen eyelet sundress and leather sandals. She didn't wear the dress often, but when she did, people commented on how it made her eyes pop.

That decided, she packed her backpack with everything she'd need for the day: her laptop; jeans and a blue "cattle dog, official dog of the coolest people on the planet" t-shirt that Ginger had given to her, just in case she needed a change of clothes; and her coffee tumbler, since it worked for water, too. Sarah figured between the cup at her house and whatever she drank at breakfast, she'd be fully caffeinated for the day. She also threw in a bag of dehydrated minnows, as the Coiffure was running low on dog treats and she figured the bag would tide them over until the new shipment arrived. Sarah bought treats for the Coiffure in bulk, as some dogs needed more than coaxing to enter the tub. A little bribery went a long way.

Jared came into the bedroom as she was zipping her backpack. He eyed the dress she had draped over a chair in their room. "You going fancy tomorrow?"

"Lottie called. She invited me...and Whiskey...to breakfast at Whispering Pines. She even cleared it with Lisa and Holly. I'm sure Whiskey will be thrilled to have more Lilly time."

At his name, Whiskey, who had curled into a ball in the middle of their king size bed, picked up his head and eyed Sarah suspiciously. "We're going visiting in the morning," she said to the dog.

He sighed and tucked his snout under his arm and closed his eyes.

"Did you get your plan done?" Sarah asked Jared as he undressed to get ready for bed.

"I did. I will read through it one more time and then send it to them tomorrow."

She moved toward him and hugged him. "That's so exciting."

He nodded his head and then said, "It is. And I feel like it is only the beginning."

"Of course," Sarah said. "You'll start with shows in Prague and then you'll have offers in Berlin, New York, London, Copenhagen, Tokyo, Shanghai, and all of the big artsy cities in the world. Just don't forget about us...the little people." She kissed his cheek.

"Never," he said. He went into the bathroom to brush his teeth and wash his face. When he emerged he asked, "You coming to bed? Gonna read for a bit?"

"A bit. But I need to get up early...not quite as early as you, but close. I need to walk Whiskey and be at the inn by six-thirty."

"That is earlier than usual for you. You setting an alarm for four-thirty or five?"

"I'm compromising at four-forty-five. I figure coffee and showering and dressing will take fifteen to twenty minutes. The walk will take thirty, Coming home to do my hair and my face will take another fifteen to twenty."

"That puts you at an hour. It'll take fifteen, maybe twenty minutes to drive there. So you could get up at five or even five-fifteen." He slid between the sheets and turned out the lamp on his nightstand. The two bedroom lamps had come from Jared's place and replaced Sarah's plain ones she had inherited from her grandmother. Jared's lamp bases looked like a desert sunset in teals and peaches and pinks. Sarah fell in love with them at first sight.

"But I hate to rush. And you know that once the beast and I get outside in the morning, he could launch a sniff fest and take forever or get his business over with quickly and want to get back home for treats and breakfast."

Jared kissed her forehead. "True. For a dog who likes his habits, he can be unpredictable." He grinned at her.

Sarah said to Whiskey, "Hey, let's do a last call, boy."

Whiskey popped from curled to standing on the bed, took a flying leap onto the rug, and raced from the room with Sarah jogging behind him to keep up. When she opened the back door, he bolted into the yard all the way to the fence where Sarah barely caught a flash of orange and white fur zip into the field next to her house. "Mozart outsmarted you again," Sarah said.

Whiskey peed against a fence post and then sniffed around the yard, turned a few competing directions, before finally squatting his back legs and doing his business.

"Good boy," Sarah said, as he trotted back into the house and straight into the bedroom.

Sarah locked the back door and padded in her bare feet back to her bedroom. She snuggled under her duvet next to Whiskey—Yes, he was in the middle between her and Jared—and opened the mystery novel she was reading. She read a few pages, but found her mind drifting to her real-life mysteries: the burglaries of the houses, the burglary of the antique store, and the murder of Micas Brighton. Originally Sarah thought all of the burglaries were related, but now she wasn't so sure. Her gut said the safe, computer, hard drive, and paintings were deliberately chosen and the cause for the break-in. In regards to the houses and the stuff stolen, it felt petty, random, and almost amateurish. A professional thief wouldn't steal just an item or two when there were plenty of other things to steal.

Was it young people playing tricks? Were the homeowners targeted for a reason Sarah hadn't yet uncovered? Or were they crimes of opportunity, of unlocked doors and open windows?

Sarah couldn't see it and she couldn't connect the dots. She needed more information. She was missing something big, but she didn't have any idea what that was.

John Beams' warning to her flashed in her mind. Would befriending and helping Lottie Brighton put her at risk? Surely seeing the crime scene while helping pack up her father's worldly possessions wasn't the same as investigating. And if she stumbled across something material and important, that was just chance, right? Besides, if she saw or learned anything pertinent to the investigations, Sarah would immediately share it with the police.

She reassured herself with those thoughts and assuaged her conscience. Sarah closed her book since she had been on the same two pages for at least ten minutes. She placed it on her nightstand, got up to pee one last time, turned off the lamp, slid back under the duvet, and shut her eyes. Jared's breath was steady, signaling he was sound asleep.

Whiskey snored lightly and repositioned himself on the bed.

When Sarah finally fell asleep, she dreamed of Micas Brighton kneeling and trussed up like a turkey pleading for his life from a black leather gloved, gun pointing faceless villain. Over and over again, he begged, "Don't kill me. I'll tell you everything you want to know. Just don't kill me. I have a daughter. I'll tell you everything." But the gunman's heart was as hard as coal. The bullet flew from the Glock into Micas' skull and knocked him onto his side. Sarah let loose a scream and woke herself up.

Jared's hand was rubbing her arm and shoulder. "Shhh, it's okay. You're okay. You're safe, Sarah. Whiskey and I are here. You are safe."

"It was horrible. So horrible. I saw Micas die in my dream." Sarah was frowning and her eyes were unfocused and far away. "He didn't want to die. He begged not to. He was so afraid." Tears rolled down her cheeks. Jared climbed over the pillows around the dog and wrapped his arms around her. He kissed the hair at the crown of her head. He held her until she calmed and the tears stopped flowing.

Sarah slipped from his arms and sought a Kleenex in the bathroom. She blew her nose, hating how stuffed up she got every time she cried. Looking at her puffy eyes in the mirror, she reminded herself that what she saw was only a dream.

When she crawled back into bed and spooned Whiskey, who was still in the middle of the bed, she apologized to Jared for waking him.

"No apologies necessary, Sarah. Partnership is being present for each other. I love you. Now let's both try to get some rest." He leaned over the dog and kissed her softly on the lips.

The alarm came too early for Sarah. Jared's alarm had gone off at three-thirty as usual and had woken her up, and she struggled to go back to sleep so by the time the trilling started at four-forty-five, Sarah was frustrated and wanted to whip her phone across the room. Whiskey side-eyed her and sighed, like he couldn't believe she would be so rude by waking him.

Since he clearly wasn't ready to go outside, she left him in bed and headed for the shower. When she was finished, dressed, and her hair had been dried, she wandered into the kitchen for some coffee. She poured a cup into her to-go tumbler though she figured the only way she'd get through the day was with a caffeine IV. At the front door she called, "Whiskey, let's go for a walk." He came tearing out of the bedroom like a tiger was hot on his heels.

She opened the front door and he bolted through without slowing his gait. Sarah shuffled after him, cursing her sandals for making her walk slower than when she wore her sneakers. "Wait up, dog," she said, but not too loudly as she didn't want to wake her neighbors.

About fifty yards up their street, Whiskey stopped and lifted his leg on some weeds. He streamed urine with the power of a racehorse, and when he was finished, he looked at Sarah with relief on his face. He waited for her to catch up, and then walked by her side up to the park.

Since it was still mostly dark, the park was deserted. Whiskey picked up a scent trail of something and he followed his nose to the evergreen that was planted as the replacement Cottageville holiday tree after an arsonist had incinerated the decades-old one. Sarah broke into a light jog, attempted to keep up with him, but her sandals, definitely not made for running, flapped against the ground with every hurried step, threatening to trip her up. Each stride became a battle between her willpower and her cute but impractical footwear.

A glint of gold caught her eye, a soft shimmer of moonlight bouncing off something partially buried in the needles and soil. Squatting down so as not to dirty her dress, Sarah used her fingertips to brush away the coating of debris. Her breath caught. It was a wedding band, large enough in diameter that it was mostly likely a man's. Sarah turned on her phone flashlight and searched the area to see if anything else was around the base of the tree. But all she saw was organic matter.

She slid the ring onto her thumb for safekeeping and said to Whiskey, "Come on, boy. We need to get home. I don't want to be late for breakfast."

His ears perked at one of his favorite words. He ran a circle around her and then nudged her ankle to get her moving toward their house and his meal. "You're too funny," Sarah told him.

When they returned home, Sarah prepared Whiskey's breakfast and while he inhaled his food, she washed the ring over the kitchen sink after making sure the drain was plugged. Once the dirt was gone, the gold band sparkled though scratches were visible on the outside and the inside, making the gold look brushed. Sarah turned the ring in the light over the sink, searching the interior of the band for any engraving, hoping to find a clue to reconnect the ring to its owner. The band was stamped inside with "14K" and to the right of that, barely noticeable, was etched "I <3 U, BRD."

Sarah frowned, wondering who BRD, which her mind pronounced as *bird*, was.

CHAPTER 15

Twenty-five minutes later, Sarah drove her green, old-school Jeep up the long driveway of Whispering Pines. After she parked, she held open the big wooden door of the inn for Whiskey, who was greeted by a hello from Lisa and a nudge from Lilly's big head. The harlequin Great Dane was almost double the height of Whiskey, who acted like a bumbling nerd around a leggy, supermodel. He trailed after her toward the back of the bed and breakfast.

"Don't worry about him," Lisa said. "She'll take him through the dog door and outside to hunt squirrels and rabbits."

"I hope they don't catch anything," Sarah said. She cringed at the thought of either dog biting into a living animal.

"Lilly hasn't yet, but she certainly gives some critters exercise they probably don't want." Lisa chuckled.

"As long as that's all it is," Sarah said.

"If you'll follow me, I believe Lottie is already in the dining room." Lisa's heels clicked on the hardwood floors as she led the way. She was the most dressed up Sarah had ever seen. Lisa wore a navy pants suit with a white shell underneath and she had a pearl brooch on her lapel.

"You look amazing, by the way," Sarah said.

"Thank you. We belong to a state-wide inn association. I was elected president last year, and our lunch meeting is today. The meetings give me an excuse to put on my power suit and remind myself why my life is so much better since leaving Wall Street." She grinned showing shiny white teeth.

"Oh, I had no idea that's what you used to do," Sarah said.

Lisa's grin grew wider. "Why? Because I usually look like a granola from Oregon?"

Sarah chuckled and admitted, "Umm, kind of. I mean, I've mostly seen you in hiking boots or gardening clothes."

They had reached a big open room with scatters of round tables with chairs for two and four. Lottie sat at the far table, facing the backyard, with her back to the open doorway Sarah and Lisa walked through.

Sarah could see the dogs racing around the acreage whose perimeter was framed by a split rail fence. She placed a hand lightly on Lottie's shoulder to signify her presence before sitting in the chair opposite the woman.

Lisa inquired if Sarah needed coffee, to which she replied, "Black, please."

When Lisa stepped away, Lottie said, "Sarah, thank you very much for meeting me." She wore white shorts, a pastel blue short sleeve sweater, and tan leather sandals. Sarah noted that her legs were strong, like a runner's and her toenails were unpainted.

"My pleasure," Sarah said, as Lisa returned with her coffee and a refill for Lottie.

"Do you both want eggs this morning? We have a lion's mane mushroom, herb, and goat cheese omelet with sides of potatoes and salad, and wheat, rye, or sourdough toast. I recommend the sourdough as we make it in house. Otherwise, we have yogurt, granola, and fruit."

"Wow," Sarah said. "That omelet sounds fancy and delicious. And homemade sourdough is divine. Thank you."

"Sounds good to me, too," Lottie said.

After Lisa left, Lottie said, "I have to be candid. I had heard about you before I met you."

"Oh?" Sarah's eyebrows raised.

"My father spoke about you, and he sent me the articles in the *Courier*, from when you were awarded Citizen of the Year and the couple that came out about you helping the police solve crime."

"Oh wow. Okay..." Sarah wasn't sure why he would do such a thing as they had barely met. She took a sip of coffee and waited for Lottie to go on, and it was as if she had read Sarah's mind.

"I know you didn't really know each other. At least that's what he told me. But he saw your curiosity and determination to follow through until you had answers similar to what he had done his whole life in the art world. He enjoyed and excelled at solving mysteries, like whether some artifact that was unearthed was as old as people thought or if a painting found in an attic or in the walls of an old building was really one of the great masters."

Sarah looked into Lottie's eyes as she said, "I'm honored that he'd think that."

"He said you had spunk." Her eyes welled with tears. "And that if anything suspicious ever happened to him in Cottageville, to make sure I talked to you."

"Chief James and his team are super competent," Sarah said.

"Oh, my dad never doubted that. He said that while the small town didn't have the resources a big city did and some things had to be handled by the county or the state, that the Cottageville P.D. was first-rate at what they do."

"And yet they couldn't prevent the death of your dad," Sarah said just above a whisper.

A single tear rolled down Lottie's face. "True...but I'm unsure anyone could have done that." She pinched her lips together. "I'm a strong believer in fate." She left the statement hanging.

Steamy plates of food were placed in front of them and the omelet and potatoes were Insta-worthy. Sarah wanted to take a photo but didn't want to seem like *that* person so she refrained. Instead, she used her fork to dig in. After swallowing the first taste-bud blowing bite, she asked, "Was Micas working on anything in particular? Do you know?"

"Some contract work for a museum in Texas, his own research. Even though he was officially retired, he still liked to write his papers and publish in the journals. And on our last call he said the Maslows bought some paintings at an estate sale and had asked him to authenticate them."

Sarah stopped with a bite of fluffy omelet halfway to her mouth. "And was he able to?"

"I don't know. Over the last two years they've brought him a number of things to assess. But I'm not sure if he had the time to determine if the paintings were really the works of Grant Wood."

Immediately an alarm bell went off in Sarah's head. That wasn't the artist Mrs. Maslow said. Sarah was familiar with Grant Wood. She hadn't been familiar with the guy whose name she couldn't remember but that started with an F she thought that Mrs. Maslow said.

"Grant Wood," Sarah parroted in thought. "Didn't he do 'American Gothic'?"

"Yes. Most people know the painting but not necessarily his name. He's from this state. That's one reason my father wanted to be here. To research more about his life and work, maybe even write a book about him."

"My boyfriend, Jared, is an artist, though his work is more commercial art than fine art."

"Cool. I studied art, too, but prefer contemporary and more avant-garde art than my father."

"Can you think of any reason someone would want to kill your father?"

Lottie held Sarah's eyes for a few seconds before she said, "The only thing I've been able to decide is that not everyone is happy with the truth. You know that television program *Antique Roadshow*?"

"The one where people find things in their barns or in their attics and then the hosts tell them if it is worth anything?"

"Exactly. It's human nature, for some people, to think the best and build it up in their heads that what they have found is going to change their lives. Like the beauty of the piece isn't enough. They want it to be worth something, to have bragging rights, or to cash it out to buy whatever shiny object they have their eyes and heart set on. Sometimes my father had to be the bearer of bad news. A museum was swindled by a forger. A small house planned to auction off a casting, not the final piece like they thought. That kind of thing."

"So an assessment on authenticity that doesn't go as planned could mean the business spent a lot of money on nothing or that it won't make what it thought it would?" Sarah ate the last bit of potato on her plate.

"Exactly. Or a family who passed down to three generations a John Singer Sargent painting comes to find out their grandfather sold the original years ago and what they have is a very high end replica... painted by someone else entirely."

"Wow. That'd be a bone too big to swallow, especially to learn granddad was a liar and maybe a cheat." Sarah smirked.

"So you can understand how..." Lottie's voice trailed off and tears streamed down her cheeks.

Sarah reached across the table and held her hand while she cried.

When Lottie's tears ceased, Sarah let go of her hand. Then Lottie surprised Sarah by saying, "What popped into my head and almost out my mouth was 'So you can understand why someone may have wanted to shoot the messenger' but then I realized that may actually be what happened." She audibly sighed.

"Did you tell any of this to the police?"

"They asked questions about my dad's work, and I explained what he did and how it upset people or companies sometimes. But I didn't say it to them the way I just said it to you."

"Do you know if your father's house was burgled? Or did it look like someone did a search? I didn't hear anything about that. The local gossip was focused on...his death." Sarah almost said "the killing" but caught herself thinking that sounded too cold.

"I'm not sure about a search, but the police asked if he had a computer or a tablet or other electronics. His phone was found in the kitchen, which is where he died. But his computer, tablet, and any peripherals or old portable hard drives weren't there."

Hmm, Sarah thought, *just like at the Maslows.*

"Had you met the Maslows before yesterday?"

"No. My dad had talked about them, said Peter knew about coins and his wife had collected stamps and liked old books. That's what got them into the antique business. He said much of their knowledge was self-taught, which was why he was trying to help them out. I reached out to them when I got to town since he had just worked for them over the weekend. I thought maybe..." Her voice trailed off again and she looked wistful. After a moment, she continued, "I guess I thought maybe they'd know something or could help me make sense of it all. But they don't really have answers to my questions. She's tried to hug me more than I'm comfortable with, and he bumbles like he doesn't know what to say." Her hand flew to her mouth and her eyes enlarged like she was now worried about what she said.

"It's okay," Sarah said. "I barely know the Maslows, but I could totally see Glenda trying to mother you. Speaking of which…"

"She's been gone a number of years. And I was an only child."

Sarah nodded her head once. "And as for him, he's always struck me as a bit gruff and…maybe uncultured is the best way to put it. Though that makes me sound elitist." Sarah frowned. "But seriously, say whatever you want about whomever you want. I promise to be a vault."

"Thank you." Lottie took a sip from her cup.

"So, does your father own the house? I thought I remembered a for sale sign on it a few years ago."

"He does. Outright."

"Do you know if you will sell it?"

"I will have to. My life is in Los Angeles, not here. Plus…" Tears filled her eyes again,

"Plus who wants the reminder," Sarah filled in.

Lottie flashed her a grimace and then a forced smile that didn't reach her eyes. "True. But I'm also not sure who wants to buy a house that now has this history."

"I'm off Saturday and Sunday and so is my assistant. If you can access the house then, would you like us to help you clean it and clean it out? I inherited my grandmother's house here in Cottageville when she died, and my parents and I had to go through her things and determine what to keep, what to pitch, and what to donate. I know how emotionally trying it can be, not to mention a ton of physical work. I'm happy to help." In her head, Sarah also thought that would give her the opportunity to look for clues as to why Micas was shot and who could have shot him.

"Thank you. I appreciate your offer. I should have the keys by tomorrow or Sunday. I'll text or call to confirm."

Sarah looked at her phone for the time and realized she needed to get to work. "I hate to cut this short, but I really must go." She signaled to Lisa for the check, but Lottie insisted she was buying. "Thank you so much," Sarah said. "And feel free to call if you need anything. Oh, and Jared said you're coming to dinner tomorrow night. Six o'clock?"

"Sounds good. What should I bring?"

"Just yourself is fine. Everything else he's taking care of." Sarah smiled. "I'll text you the address." Then she left the dining room to find her dog and get on the road to the Coiffure, where she knew Emily was waiting.

Twenty minutes later, she pulled into a parking space in front of her business and her eyes zeroed in on what looked like a brown leather photo album sitting on the sidewalk between the Italian restaurant and the Coiffure. Sarah slid down from the Jeep and waited for Whiskey to exit before she shut the vehicle's door. Then instead of heading inside to Emily, she walked the four feet down the sidewalk and squatted to examine the book. The cover had black leather trim around rich brown cowhide on the front, back, and spine. It was sumptuous and tactile under Sarah's fingertips. Sarah flipped the front to the left and her breath caught when round pockets filled with coins stared back at her. *What the heck? Why was a coin collection on the sidewalk? And was this the one that had been stolen?* Sarah realized that her prints were now on it.

She pulled out her phone and took a picture of it as it sat on the pavement. And then she called Chief James and reported what she had found...just in case it was the missing collection.

CHAPTER 16

As she waited for him or one of his officers to arrive, Sarah stuck her head into the Coiffure door and said, "Hey, Em. What time did you get here?" Whiskey pushed past her to get inside.

Emily admitted she arrived early, at seven-thirty, and then walked to Java and Juice to get her coffee and their lunch salads.

"Thank you for doing that," Sarah said. "Did you notice a leather book that looks like a photo album on the sidewalk between us and the restaurant?"

"No. There wasn't one. I walked down that part of the sidewalk twice. Why?"

"Well, it's here now, The police are on their way. I think it may be the stolen coin collection, though I have no idea why anyone would leave it on the sidewalk."

Emily came to the door and stuck her head out, eying the book. "Hmm. That definitely wasn't there before. It's so strange. Did you move it?"

"I opened the front cover and then shut it once I realized what it was. But I didn't pick it up."

"It's weird how square it is with the sidewalk. Looks equidistant from the edge of the pavement on the left and right, or what for the book is the top and bottom."

"Excellent point, Em. Clearly someone placed it there. They didn't drop it."

"Yes, and someone who values preciseness. Nice dress, by the way."

"Thank you." Sarah handed her backpack to Emily to put inside, just as a black and white police cruiser parked at the curb. Officer Grimes greeted Sarah. "You can't help but stumble over clues, can you?" She grinned at her friend.

"Sometimes I find them, but just as often, they find me." Sarah beamed at the truth of her statement. "And if I were a betting person, I'd take odds on this being the stolen coin collection, though I have no idea why someone would discard it in this fashion."

"Did you touch it?"

"Yes. It's how I knew it was coins and not photos. My prints are on file."

"Yes, they are. Did you move it?"

"Only opened the front cover and shut it. The book's location is exactly how I found it at a quarter after eight. Emily walked this sidewalk twice between seven-thirty and my arrival and said the book wasn't there then."

"Did you look around to see if anything else had been dumped here?"

"No, I didn't. But that reminds me. Hang on a second." Sarah went into the Coiffure and searched in an outer pocket of her backpack until she found the gold band. Then she popped back out to where Candace was taking photos of the coin collection and the surrounding area.

"I found this in the park this morning under the new evergreen." She handed the ring to Officer Grimes.

Candance held it up to the morning sunlight. "Sparkly."

"Engraved with initials, RBD, no wait, that's not right. Bird. BRD."

"As in Benjamin Robert Davis. Well done, Sarah."

"Huh? That's Bobby's father's wedding band?"

"It is indeed. He'll be so happy to have it back...once it isn't being used as evidence. You said you found it under the tree?"

"Yes, it was partially buried, but the moonlight reflected on the gold and twinkled, which is why it caught my eye. I just figured someone lost it in the park. As in maybe it fell off or had been pocketed and fell out."

Candace's eyes narrowed at the ring and her gaze went from it to the coin collection and back again. "It's weird, but it seems like whoever stole these things wanted them found. Which doesn't make any sense. Why take things and return them? Or make them easy to find at least?"

"Maybe the person who took them had no way to sell them. Or realized it wouldn't be as easy as they originally thought. I mean, don't you guys send notices to all of the pawn shops and stuff to be on the lookout for stolen items?"

"We do. And we did with these."

"So maybe they realized the items were too hot."

"Maybe. I'm gonna finish up bagging these things and investigating the area, and then I'll go search the tree. Thank you for finding this, Sarah, and for calling it in."

"Of course. Please let me know if you stumble across any of the other items."

Officer Grimes said nothing but sent Sarah a smile.

Whiskey greeted Sarah when she entered the Coiffure. She grabbed her denim paw print apron from the hook by the door. Emily asked how the breakfast went, and Sarah filled her in, asking if she and one of the T's was available tomorrow to help clean Micas Brighton's house, even though a few days ago Emily had said she would.

"Umm," Em said. "Does it still look like a crime scene?"

"I guess. But I don't know for sure."

"I will help box up books and his things, and I'm sure I can get Travis or Taylor to come with me if they aren't working, but I don't want to see blood or brain matter or whatever gore happens from a shooting." The color had drained from Emily's face.

"He was killed in the kitchen, Lottie said. So just avoid the kitchen."

"Umm, okay."

"I'm still not sure if tomorrow will be the day, but it seems like it. Are you available Sunday, too?"

"Mostly since it's the holiday weekend."

"I'll let you know what the plan is once I hear from Lottie. I appreciate your willingness to help. So it looks like we have a Newfoundland, a yorkie, and Merlin the Maltese on the schedule today."

"Oh yeah, Ben texted that he and Apollo are running a few minutes late. Something about a combine falling off a truck and blocking the state route. That's why they aren't here yet."

"Huh. I didn't hear any sirens this morning."

"Maybe it wasn't considered an emergency. So did Candace say that the coin collection was part of the theft?"

"She didn't confirm or deny. I found a ring this morning in the park, too. A wedding band. It was inscribed, and she did say that it belonged to Bobby's dad."

"Do you think Daphne's shoes will pop up at the playground or her leather coat will magically appear somewhere?" Emily took a long pull from her coffee cup.

"I have no idea. But I am a bit suspicious about..." Sarah went silent trying to figure out exactly why two of the things that were stolen showing up rattled her. Finally, she said, "...the person's intent, both in stealing the items and then making them reappear like a twisted magic trick." Sarah wondered if the Maslows' computer or paintings would reappear, too, but she doubted it. She wasn't sure the theft at their antique store was related to the others. Her intuition said it was more likely, based on what was stolen from the store and from Micas Brighton's house, that those two crimes were related. But she lacked any proof.

The green door of the Coiffure opened, interrupting her thoughts. Apollo lumbered into the waiting area and greeted Whiskey with a big slurp. "I'm sorry, Whiskey," Ben said, wiping Whiskey's head with the hand towel he constantly carried. Newfies, like many breeds with large loose lips and jowls, were almost continual slobberers, and Apollo was no different. Ben had a small collection of towels, in his car, in his pockets, and in every room of his house, to try and keep his clothing, furniture, and rugs from being drenched in drool—it was a never ending battle.

"Don't worry about it, Ben," Sarah said.

Emily had grabbed Apollo's leash and was encouraging Whiskey to accompany him to the walk-in tub.

"Please give us four hours," Sarah said.

"See you after lunch. Thank you." Ben wore khaki cargo shorts and a navy polo shirt with work boots. Sarah realized she was unsure of what he did for a living.

When she was washing the back end of Apollo while Emily scrubbed the front and Whiskey assumed the role of supervisor, she asked Em if she knew.

"I don't. He gives off a retired firefighter vibe, but he's not old enough to be retired."

Sarah thought for a few moments and said, "Maybe retired military? I think the firefighter vibe is because he walks straight-spined, like he's a hero or disciplined or something."

"Maybe. But he's got a soft heart. Especially for this big guy." Emily scratched at the dog's ear.

Rinsing the one hundred and fifty pound dog took a very long time. Its dense coat did not release shampoo suds easily. But once the water ran clear, Sarah and Emily wrapped the dog in two big, absorbent Turkish cotton bath sheets before leading him to the grooming area.

Sarah had laid out two of each item: their largest pin brush, an undercoat rake, a slicker brush, and a mat splitter, Just as they were about to start the brushing process, with one of them on each side of the dog, Sarah's phone chimed with an incoming text. She pulled it from her apron's pocket and said aloud to Emily: "Candace went to the tree in the park where I found the ring. A box of Daphne's expensive shoes had been placed up in the branches."

'So they've now recovered three of the items that were stolen." Emily's eyes narrowed. "There's no note or anything with anything, is there?"

"I found no note with the ring or the coin collection."

"It's just so weird, Sarah, like someone is playing a game."

Emily's comment caused firecrackers to explode in Sarah's brain. *A game. That's exactly what the taking of a few items here and a couple items there seemed like. Someone supporting a drug habit or needing quick cash wouldn't cherry-pick items. Stealing as much as possible of value would have netted the thief the most money. But if the items showed up one by one and were sort of returned, that netted the thief nothing but the adrenaline rush of entering places he, she, or they weren't legally supposed to, and the rush of returning things around town without being seen. That definitely seemed like a game...out of boredom or curiosity or even challenge. As in how much could the person get away with?*

As they worked their brushes through Apollo's coat and undercoat, Sarah asked Emily, "If you were going to break into houses and take a few things, just because you could, or you wanted to see what you could get away with, how old would you be?"

"What?" Em's eyes met hers over the dog's broad back.

"I don't think the people or person who broke into the houses was a drug addict or a professional thief or even vicious like trying to get back at the few people whose houses were entered. Especially now that their things are reappearing. You're right in that it seems like a game or someone trying to make a statement, though I'm not sure what. So, if my assumptions are correct, how old would you think the person is behind this? Does it seem like the work of a teenager or an adult?"

"I don't see a teenager breaking into an antique store, Sarah. Too boring."

"Could you see them stealing a coin collection and the other things taken, as maybe a joke?"

Emily squinted her eyes as she worked a small mat out of Apollo's black fur. "I could see a teenager maybe pocketing something here and there from the homes of their friends. Kind of like that *Trinkets* show. But the things taken in the recent burglaries don't scream teen to me. The items taken aren't cool enough."

"That's what I thought," Sarah said. "It feels adult. And originally I thought it might be more than one person working in tandem, but since things started popping up this morning, it feels like a solo job."

"Why?" Emily asked Sarah. To Apollo, she said, "Hang on, big guy, you have a bit of a mess here. I'm gonna be as gentle as possible, but we have to work this knot out. I don't want to cut it and leave you with a bald patch."

"For one, it would be easier for one person to sneak around placing things precisely on the sidewalk than for two people. Much greater likelihood of being seen."

"Yes, but if they are locals, we might not even notice what they are doing. I swear I say hi to people every day and then don't remember I've seen them. Or I don't see people for days but think I have. It's part of small-town living where it all runs together."

"Maybe," Sarah said. "I also think getting two or more people to agree on stealing and then sort-of returning the items would be difficult. You know, one might want to keep the ring as a trophy, or trinket, like the show was called."

"That's true. Look at *The Bling Ring*. Those people that stole from Paris Hilton and the others, one sold stuff, one kept the stuff, I think. And one wasn't as secretive as the others. I think that's part of why they got caught."

"So if you are going to steal and make sure no one tells on you, it's best to do it by yourself and tell no one."

"True, Sarah. But what if the returning of the stuff is just as big of a taunt as the taking of it?"

"Do you mean like you didn't catch me when I stole it, and now you aren't catching me while I return it?"

"Maybe. I mean, why else would you take stuff and then put the pieces around town?"

"Why indeed, unless you were making a statement or playing a trick or a game. I guess we'll have to wait and see if everything turns up or if a specific item gets kept. And of course, if the person gets caught."

"Sarah, if the person returns everything, will they still be charged with theft?"

"They still broke and entered...even if the door or window was unlocked. And they still stole. But I don't know how the police will handle everything. It's a strange case, that's for sure."

"I'm ready to start the blow drying now," Emily said. "Are you good?"

Sarah trimmed one last bit of scraggly fur on Apollo's belly near his right back leg. "I am now." She picked up the blow dryer from her side of the dog, and she and Emily started at the front with the dryer in one hand and the brush in the other and got to work on the long process of getting the water out of the newfie's two coats.

Two hours later when Apollo was done and had been picked up by Ben, Emily and Sarah ate barbecue chicken salads and flipped through their email and social media accounts. Emily broke the silence by saying, "Hey, Sarah, someone just posted on the Cottageville message board saying they were in the library when Chief James came in to retrieve a long leather coat. The poster thought it was odd since it's way too hot for a leather coat in July. But then they overheard the Chief thank Carole for calling, since the coat was one of the stolen objects."

"Wait. Someone put it in the library? Does the post say where?"

"No." Emily swiped her finger up like she was checking the comments.

"So now we have four things sort of returned. And all on the same day. It's almost as if the person is trying to return them as quickly as they stole them."

"It's been more than a few hours," Emily said.

"Since each item has been found, yes. But I wonder if they ran from place to place hiding the items in plain sight."

The door of the Coiffure opened and Whiskey ran to his favorite mailman for a head scratch.

"Hi, Hank," Sarah said.

Hank wore his usual straw hat, USPS-issued blue short sleeve shirt and gray shorts with a stripe on the side. His mailbag was slung across his body. "Package for you, Sarah."

He placed a brown paper wrapped square box on the counter, along with a few pieces of mail in business size envelopes, before retracing his steps to the door.

"Thank you. Have a great afternoon," Sarah called after him.

Sarah inspected the package. Her name and the address for the Coiffure had been typed on a label which had been adhered to the paper. The postmark was Cottageville, and a return address was absent. Sarah's heart sank to her belly as the package triggered flashbacks to the threats she had received not too many months ago.

She put her ear near the box, listening for ticking.

She heard none.

So she donned rubber gloves so she didn't add prints, just in case, and picked up the box and shook it. Something inside moved around and sounded heavy as it slid into the side. Maybe whatever it was lacked air pillows or other packaging.

Sarah debated calling the police or fire departments, but when

Emily asked, "Aren't you going to open it?" Sarah decided to go for it.

She used a kitchen knife to slice the paper on the side of the box. She slid the cardboard box, recycled from an Amazon delivery and devoid of any labels or addresses, from the paper. The box wasn't sealed. Its flaps were folded with corners under each other.

Sarah stuck her index finger under the flap and pulled, and the corners came free. Sarah's breath caught at the contents: a stack of cash with a rubber band around its middle and a handgun. A computer printed index card contained the words: I STOLE BECAUSE I COULD. COTTAGEVILLE RESIDENTS ARE TOO TRUSTING.

"Call the police," Sarah instructed Emily, whose mouth was agape as she stared into the box.

CHAPTER 17

Emily disconnected the phone and said, "Officer Grimes is on her way. Why do you think the gun and money were sent to you, Sarah? I mean, why you instead of to the police station?"

"I don't know. But if I had to guess, the sender either knew I was trustworthy enough to turn it over to law enforcement or sending a package to me wouldn't trigger any alarms at the post office, like maybe one addressed to the police HQ would, or maybe both." Sarah closed the flaps on the box just in case their next clients came through the door. She didn't want anyone to see inside the box as she knew word would spread faster than a wildfire in a drought-stricken prairie.

Within five minutes, the black and white patrol car was parked at the curb and Candace walked into the Coiffure saying, 'Sarah, we have to stop meeting like this."

Whiskey ran to the door to say hello.

"Very funny," Sarah said. "I'd love for people to stop involving me in their crimes."

"No, you wouldn't, Nancy Drew wanna-be," Candace shot back. "You love this stuff."

"Well, true, but in this case, it feels like I, and the rest of Cottageville, is being toyed with. Check out the note." Still wearing the gloves, Sarah pushed the box forward toward the officer.

"Well, that's one way to make a statement. And that certainly looks like the make and model of the gun that was stolen. I take it you didn't help yourself to any of the cash?" Candace grinned in a crooked, lopsided way that let Sarah and Em know she was joking.

"Never even touched the contents of the box," Sarah said.

"And I didn't even touch the box itself let alone its contents," Emily added, then frowned. Her frown tugged at the corners of her mouth like invisible weights, creasing her brow and casting a shadow over her usually curious expression. "Is that gun loaded?"

"Oh my gosh. I hope not," Sarah exclaimed. "I mean, it could have accidentally gone off while Hank carried it or I when I shook the box."

Donning thin latex gloves, Candace pulled the revolver from the box by its worn handle. With a flick of her thumb, she popped the cylinder out and tilted the gun. The chambers were all empty.

Sarah released a breath she didn't consciously know she was holding.

"So, Hank dropped this off when?" Candace pulled a small notebook from her pocket along with a pen.

"Maybe two minutes before Emily called nine-one-one."

"Which would have been how many minutes ago?" Candace looked down at her watch.

"Within the past ten minutes," Sarah said.

Candace moved the box and its contents into a big evidence bag and sealed it. "Anything in the rest of your mail?"

Sarah quickly flipped through the four envelopes. "Electric bill. ValPak of coupons. Business insurance bill. Flyer for an open house for a home for sale one street over. That's it."

"Okay. I'll go now before too many of our fine citizens stoke the rumor mill regarding why I was near your business twice in one day."

"That fire is probably already raging," Sarah said.

"Most likely. Bye, Emily. Take good care of Sarah, Whiskey." And with those parting words, Officer Grimes was out the door.

A few moments later, their next client entered and since it was a small dog, Emily asked, "Hey, Sarah, did you want to go talk to Carole at the library? I know you missed her the other day, and well, now that they found Daphne's coat..." Em left the rest of the sentence remain unsaid.

"If you're sure you are okay here. I won't be long." Sarah already had her apron loop over her head. She held her phone in her hand and said, "Call me, if anything comes up. Whiskey, stay with Em."

Sarah saw Carole Binds at the circulation desk as soon as she walked into the air conditioned space. Carole met her eyes with a smile, but waited to speak until Sarah was right in front of her. "I wondered how long it would take you to show up. I figured as soon as you heard about the coat, I'd be seeing you." Her eyes were kind and full of mischief. Her glasses and clothes were bright and stylish.

"This is actually a repeat of an attempt to talk to you a couple of days ago, but yes, I'll admit I'm intrigued by the appearance of Daphne's coat. Where exactly was it found?"

"Hanging from the hook on the back of a bathroom stall, of all places." Carole's lips squished together in a straight line.

"Men's or women's?"

"Neither. The family unisex bathroom we installed recently. It has a lovely changing table and a wide door that is stroller and wheelchair friendly."

"Interesting," Sarah said.

"What did you want a few days ago?"

"To ask you if Micas Brighton did any research here or if you ordered him any special books or journals through the interlibrary loan." Sarah paused, and then added, "And Emily said to remind you she was still interested in a mystery novel with a..." Sarah couldn't remember what Em had said was on the front cover.

Fortunately for her, Carole said, "I have that book right here," and pulled the novel from under the counter. It had a Post-it note on the cover with "Emily Colt" written on it. "Would you like to check it out on her behalf or should I add it to her account and you can take it to her?"

"Either way...unless she accumulates a lot of fines," Sarah joked.

"Not since she was seven," Carole chuckled.

"About Micas," Sarah prompted.

"Yes, he did some research, but mostly he used connections he had to university library systems and places with much bigger inventories than ours. But he was fascinating to talk to and we discussed art for dozens of hours during his time in Cottageville."

Sarah figured her next question was a bit of a long shot, but she asked it anyway. "Did he check out any books or do research about things unrelated to art?"

"Do you mean like did he read other nonfiction or westerns or thrillers or such?"

"Maybe. I'm trying to get a better sense of who he was, what his interests were, why someone would shoot him."

"From my experience with him, he lived and breathed all things art. I never heard him mention sports." She clicked some keys on the library's main computer and then said, "He never checked out any fiction. Not a single title. Though I know we talked about some because he had some first editions that made me envious. He was engaging and smart and quirky in the way he knew obscure facts about painters, sculptors, ceramicists, jewelers, architects, etc. who have now become part of our cultural knowledge. Names you know."

"Did he mention doing research on Grant Wood?" Sarah asked.

"Yes. He said he was planning a book."

"And did he ever mention the painter Fairfield Porter to you?"

Carole's eyes narrowed in thought. "I don't think so. But I don't know who that is so I'm not sure if he was mentioned in passing his name would have stuck."

"Have either of the Maslows been asking to see art books or anything about either Grant Wood or Fairfield Porter?"

"You mean Glenda or Peter? No. Glenda reads romances and cozy mysteries, usually with quilting or knitting or baking as themes. The only time I've ever seen Peter was when he was checking out books related to gambling. You know, self-help on being a better poker player, how to win at blackjack, how to build the best fantasy football team."

"There's actually a book on fantasy football?"

"There's a whole sports playbook series. People take that kind of thing very seriously. Too seriously, in my opinion, and it can be a way to gamble." Carole gave Sarah a pointed look like she was trying to convey something without saying the words.

"Thank you so much for your time, Carole. I appreciate you talking with me. I should really get back to work. Don't want to leave Emily alone with the dogs for too long." Sarah reached across the counter to give the librarian a hug.

"You're welcome, Sarah. I'm happy to talk to you any time. And I love your dress, by the way."

Sarah smiled. "Thank you." As she walked back to the Coiffure, she wondered if she should wear a wider range of clothing more often, instead of her daily dog t-shirt and jeans.

Emily was blow drying a dog while Merlin the Maltese awaited his turn and hung out with Whiskey in the waiting room. The two dogs were stretched out on the floor side by side, chins on their outstretched front legs. They eyed her when she entered but didn't rush to greet her.

Sarah put Emily's book on the table and then grabbed her apron from the table, slid the loop over her head, and double wrapped the ties around her waist before knotting it in a bow. "Come on, Merlin, let's get you prettied up," she said, scooping the dog off the floor. Whiskey nipped at her heels as she carried his friend to a tub.

"Learn anything, Sarah?" Emily yelled over the hum of the dryer.

Sarah relayed how the coat was found in the unisex bathroom. She said that since the library had security cameras both outside and in she was sure the police were reviewing the footage. "I did learn something that may be interesting about Peter Maslow." Sarah worked the shampoo into Merlin's white fur and the dog sighed against her fingers and closed his eyes.

"What's that?" Emily asked.

"I think he likes to gamble."

"Oh?" Emily raised her eyebrows at Sarah.

"Carole said the only books he's taken out are about poker, blackjack, and fantasy football."

"There's quite the local fantasy football league," Em said. "Taylor plays, but I don't see the appeal. And did you know that when Butch Cassava took over the bar and rebranded as Butch's Brewery, he started card games in the back room. Not sure they are legal, but my dad went with his friend once. Said the stakes were too high for him."

"I had no idea," Sarah said. She had only been in the Brewery once. Its vibe and clientele were what Gigi would have called rough around the edges. In the summer months, the bar attracted a lot of Harley riders wearing leather vests with patches of motorcycle clubs. And just last year, the place had been raided for drugs. "I wonder if Mr. Maslow goes there."

"Maybe," Emily said. "But let's face it, many people gamble

from the comfort of their own homes with their personal computers or smartphones. So many games. Slots, cards, bingo, so many ways to place bets and get promises of winning big."

"So many ways to go into debt," Sarah added. Then her words from Monday night's conversation with Jared about the industries the mafia worked in or controlled came back to her: *gambling, prostitution, the running of drugs and guns, money laundering. What if Peter Maslow had a debt to an unsavory sort and that was the reason for the break-in at their business? But that wouldn't explain why Micas Brighton was shot execution style. She had to be missing something, some crucial piece of information of how the events were related, her intuition kept saying they must be. And what did a high stakes card game in Cottageville mean? How much exactly were the stakes? And did that have any bearing on any parts of Saturday's and Monday's crimes?*

"Earth to Sarah. Come in, Sarah. Join us here again at Carter's Canine Coiffure." Emily's voice cut through the questions and clutter in Sarah's head.

"I'm with you again," she assured her assistant as she turned on the water to rinse Merlin.

"Where did you go? Did you have a nice trip?" Emily teased, a sparkle in her eye and a quirk on her lips.

"I mentally connected gambling with the mob and possibly the mob to the killing, but I couldn't complete the circle with how the mob and Micas connect or Micas and gambling connect."

"So you're left with three-quarters of a moon?" Emily laughed.

"More like a half or a quarter." Sarah tsked in disgust, then wrapped Merlin in a towel much bigger than he was.

"You could ask your new friend Lottie if her dad liked to play cards." Emily was cleaning her work station and preparing it for their next client.

"Hey, that's a great idea. I'll text her when I'm done with the grooming." Sarah got to work trimming the fur around Merlin's face and then along his belly. His human preferred for his coat not to touch the ground and for the fur around his face to seem feathered in length as opposed to Mortician Gomez one-length and straight down the sides of his face.

A few minutes to three, the door of the Coiffure opened and Sarah turned to see the welcome sight of Jared's tousled red hair and weary eyes. "Hey, love. What brings you to my humble business?" Whiskey stood on his hind legs to greet Jared.

"The coffee shop chorus sang Sarah Carter as too frequent a refrain today so I'm personally checking on your well-being. How are you? And did you really turn over things stolen to the police three times today?" Jared's eyes bore into hers.

"Stumbled across. Found on the sidewalk. Mailed directly to me."

He shook his head back and forth. "And did you open the package mailed directly to you?"

"Yes. But not immediately." She felt sure she knew what worried him. "I wore gloves and listened for ticking first." She grinned at him to try and alleviate the tension she felt emitting from him in waves.

"You know not all bombs tick, right?"

"I do." Sarah debated telling him about the clunk she heard when she shook the package but figured that wouldn't help her case so she kept that information to herself.

Instead, she said, "I love you, Jared. I didn't mean to worry you. I'm safe. Whiskey is safe. Emily is safe. Candace has everything in custody."

"Um, I think people get put into custody and those things are catalogued as evidence."

Sarah waved her hand like the terminology didn't matter because he got her point. She changed the subject to take his focus from her past actions. "Did you know Butch's Brewery has what might be illegal card games in their back room?"

Jared's eyes narrowed like he didn't like her changing the subject. "I have heard about them. It's kind of a semi-open secret in certain circles of our town."

"My dad went once," Emily piped up from the table in the back.

"Did he have fun?" Jared asked.

"Nope. Said the stakes were too high for him."

"Em, do you know what 'too high stakes' for your dad means? Are we talking twenty dollars a bet? One hundred? One thousand?" Sarah asked.

"No idea. I can ask him if you want when I get home tonight and text you the answer."

"If you think about it."

"Hey, Jared, will you drive the CJ home for me? I haven't walked enough today and Whiskey needs more exercise, too. I can give you the keys." Sarah reached into an outside zipper pocket of her backpack for them.

Jared asked, "Yes, but do you think you can avoid coming across any more stolen items on your way home?"

Sarah suddenly felt a pang of guilt for the weight the Cottageville gossip mill had put on Jared. She reached across the counter and took his head. "I will try. But it wasn't like I went out looking for any of these things. I was shocked as heck to come across the coin collection. I couldn't believe the thief would give things back. And I still don't quite understand why."

"The chatter said there was a note," Jared said quietly, and ran his free hand over his face.

"Yes. It said that the person stole because they could and that the people who live here are too trusting."

"So they stole to prove that? To what end? Would they prefer suspicious neighbors always on edge of something bad happening, like people walk through big cities always on the defensive? That's rubbish."

"I agree. How about if you and I have a date tonight? I'll be home in an hour and half or so, five at the latest, and we can leave Whiskey at home for once and I'll take you to wherever you want to go to eat. We could use some us time, and clearly, you've been worried about me all day. I didn't mean to cause you concern."

"You didn't really. It's all of the talk and the speculation and everything. You know how it goes. It starts with the truth and then by the time it's on everyone's tongues, it may be a sliver of the original facts. I shouldn't have listened to it or let it get to me." He leaned over the counter and kissed her. "And I'd love to be your date tonight. Thank you." He kissed her again, and then turned toward the door.

CHAPTER 18

"**W**here are you going to take him?" Emily asked as soon as Jared had shut the door.

"I'm not sure. My suggestion was impetuous so I haven't thought about the possibilities."

"There's that new place near the interstate, Delilah's Delights. It has a cheesy name, but the food is supposed to be awesome. It has a Mediterranean-inspired menu."

"Yeah because that makes sense in the middle of a landlocked state." Sarah smirked.

Em pulled up a menu on her phone. "Lots of things with olives and capers and olive oil. Whole grain pastas and fresh herbs, veggies, and fruits like tomatoes. Looks yummy."

"Maybe," Sarah said. "Though Jared kind of cooks like that at home. I'm thinking we should eat something we don't make at home. Like maybe pho or Thai food or even Mexican."

"Hey, there's that tapas bar by the mall. It's pretty good. Taylor and I went there last week. We had fried squid and shrimp in some kind of garlic sauce, as well as some paella. Well, we took home most of the paella as we had ordered way too much food because we wanted to try so much." Emily grinned and then smacked her lips together. "Everything was delicious. Even the squid, which if not done right can be like chewing a rubber band."

"So true," Sarah said. She threw a load of towels into the washer and started to refill the shampoo bottles on the shelves from the gallon jugs under the sinks.

"Did you need a reservation?"

"Nah. We ate at the bar. That's where all of the action is."

Emily used the broom to sweep up the dog hair in the grooming area. She continued to sweep into the other rooms since Whiskey and his friends tended to run all around. When she was done, she filled the bucket with sudsy water and grabbed the mop and cleaned every floor surface in the former house.

Sarah looked over the schedule for the following week and as she did so, her phone chimed with an incoming text from Lottie. "The Chief of Police said I could come by tomorrow morning at 8 for the keys. Can you and your friends still work tomorrow?"

"Absolutely. I wouldn't want you to be there alone," Sarah responded.

"Thank you. 9?"

"Sounds good." Sarah debated asking Lottie if her dad gambled but then thought the question would be better asked in person.

"Em, you still up for going to Micas Brighton's tomorrow? Lottie said she'll get the keys in the morning. I'm meeting her there at nine."

"I can do that. I checked earlier with the Ts and both are working tomorrow but off on Sunday."

"Okay, well if we don't get it all done tomorrow. Oh and Jared invited Lottie to our house for dinner tomorrow. Do you want to come, too? Travis can join us."

"Thanks. Can I give you a maybe or let you know closer to when we are done? I may be too tired, depending on how much stuff we need to move." Emily laughed with her eyes.

"No pressure. And of course."

"So what do I need to bring?"

"If you have any extra boxes laying around your house, like from Amazon or whatever. When Gigi died, we used a lot of boxes and garbage bags to separate what got kept, what went to the thrift store, what went to the church's clothing bank, and what got pitched."

"Okay. I'll see what we have. Packing tape then and maybe a big marker?"

"Probably."

"I'll stop and get donuts and we'll get one of those cartons of coffee in case there's none at Micas' house. And I'm sure we can have pizza or something delivered for lunch."

"Will work for food, Sarah. Oh and sugar and caffeine." Emily giggled. "Or for more Doc Martens," she added with a wicked grin.

"I'd expect nothing less."

Whiskey eyed the two of them from his perch on the waiting room sofa. He was used to the afternoon routine and their bantering. When Sarah moved the laundry from the washer to the dryer and then hung her apron the hook by the door, he stood and stretched.

"Have a great night, Em," Sarah said, carrying her backpack toward the door.

"You too, Sarah. Enjoy date night." Emily blew Sarah a kiss, which made Sarah laugh.

On the walk home, Sarah kept her eyes peeled, looking left and right and directly in front of her. She didn't want to miss one of the last three stolen items that hadn't yet been returned. At least Sarah thought three items were left: Mrs. Davis' earrings and two more pairs of Daphne's shoes, that may be Christian Louboutin, if Candace's red sole comment was correct. And she realized as she walked that she was making the assumption the thief would return those items. But even if the thief had deposited them somewhere around town, it didn't mean anyone would find them...or find them soon. Every year Mayor Trish held an Easter hunt in Cottageville Park for children under the age of ten. And every summer and fall, plastic eggs were discovered still in their hiding places...or maybe wherever an animal relocated them. Just last month Sarah had spotted a lilac colored egg in the hollow of a tree. She was sure it was leftover from the Easter egg hunt, though based on how dirty it was and how melted the chocolate candy inside the plastic shell, Sarah wasn't sure if it was from this year's festivities or a prior year's.

When she and Whiskey passed through the park on their way

to Jared, Sarah paused at that same tree and looked in the cavity, just in case the thief knew about it and had hidden the earrings or a shoe. But all she saw was remnants of insect activity. Whiskey paused with Sarah and peed at the base of the tree before leading them on their way.

Forty-five minutes later, Whiskey had been fed and had crashed for an after-dinner nap, and Jared and Sarah followed the hostess on a meandering path through high booths and low tables in the tapas restaurant. They had decided not to sit in the bar since it was packed with people and the noise volume made conversation challenging.

From one of the high, semi-circle booths came the voice of Mayor Trish. "Sarah. Jared. How great to see you. Come meet my son." Trish was dressed more casually than Sarah had ever seen her in a t-shirt and jeans, and the boy next to her had a slight dusting of acne on his forehead below dark wavy hair that could use a shampoo. He wore an Iron Man t-shirt, blue jeans, and flip flops.

"Excuse us a second," Jared said to the hostess.

She motioned to a table five feet away and said, "You'll be seated here," and then she closed that distance to put their menus at their places on their table for two.

"Thank you," Jared said, while Sarah said, "Mayor, so nice to run into you." Sarah shook her hand.

Trish said. "Cal, this is Sarah Carter, owner of Carter's Canine Coiffure and Cottageville's Citizen of the Year. And this is Jared Greene–"

Before Trish could say any more, her son interrupted with "No way. Your artwork is fire. Man, wait 'til I tell my friends." He thrust out his hand and Jared shook it. "Can I get your autograph and take a selfie?"

Jared's dimples popped, and his grin at the teen was huge. "Of course." He slid into Cal's side of the booth and sat next to him, putting his arm around his shoulders.

While Jared and Cal hammed it up for the camera and Jared acted like Cal's new BFF, Sarah listened to Trish explain out of the side of her mouth, "Callendale goes to boarding school and prefers to spend his breaks with his father in New York. But the poor dear's dad married wife number three—only eight years Cal's senior—and decided to embark on a three-month honeymoon so Cal had no choice but to come to Cottageville for the summer. I'm trying to make the best of it for both of us. But fifteen-year-olds. What can I say? He'd prefer me to leave meals at his door and not to acknowledge his presence in public." Trish shrugged.

"That's rough," Sarah said. "So I guess he hasn't joined you at Java and Juice or gone to the movie nights or the concerts either?"

"No matter how much I've begged or tried to bribe with meatball subs, which are his favorite." Trish smiled at Sarah, who looked over at Jared and Callendale, who seemed to now be recording a short video. Jared's index and middle fingers were thrown up near his face in a peace sign and he was smiling and speaking at Cal's phone.

"Hey, Jared, maybe we should let them finish their meal." Both Trish and Cal had food on their plates and the dish with paella didn't even have a spoonful out of it.

"Okay," Jared said at the same time Cal said, "Hey, Jared, I'll be in Cottageville for another month. Maybe we could hang out?" The question was asked while the teen stared down at his plate.

"We could," Jared said. "Or if you are into games, you could join us a week from Monday. A group of us get together every other week."

Cal's eyes rose to meet Jared's. "I could? That would be awesome."

"I'll provide the deets next week. Enjoy your meal and the time with your mom." Jared placed his hand on the small of Sarah's back and guided her to their table.

After the waitress had taken their order of sangria, *croquetas, tortilla de patata,* some cheese and ham, and some fried squid and had departed, Sarah admitted to Jared, "I didn't even know Mayor Trish had a son...or an ex-husband."

"Me neither, which is so weird considering everyone seems to know everything about everyone in our town. I love Cottageville, don't get me wrong, but I couldn't imagine being a teenager who's too young to drive and has no friends in the area and being told I had to be here all summer." Sincerity shown in Jared's green eyes.

"Which is why you invited him to game night." Sarah loved how compassionate and empathetic he was.

"Exactly."

Carrying a round tray, the waitress returned to their table with small glasses and the half-pitcher of sangria. She poured the fruit and wine into the glasses and gave one to each of them. "Your food will be up soon. I'll bring it as each dish is ready."

"Thank you," Jared said.

When the waitress left, Jared raised his glass to Sarah. "*¡Chinchín!* And we are celebrating because I have news."

"Tell me. Tell me," Sarah said before she took a sip from her glass.

"I love things worth celebrating." She grinned like the Cheshire cat.

"You know that proposal I sent to the gallery in Prague? They *loved* it! One of their featured artists had to back out because of a serious health issue, so guess what? They asked me to take the spot. Starting October 1st! Can you believe it Sarah?"

"Holy cow," Sarah said. "You're going to Prague this year?"

Jared raised his eyebrows at her. His eyes were wide. "*We* are going to Prague this year. You said you wanted to come so let's do this." He raised his glass again. "To seeing the Czech Republic and to meeting my fans." The wattage from his smile could have powered a city of five million people.

"Hear, hear." Sarah hoped he could see the love in her eyes. She was thrilled his dreams were coming true and her heart felt full that he wanted her on the journey with him.

The waitress arrived with their first three dishes and while they ate they discussed Jared's plan for the exhibit, the things he still needed to buy to make his vision and all of its pieces possible, and what kind of schedule he needed to adhere to to meet the deadlines."

At one point during the dinner, Sarah pulled out her phone and searched to see whether or not they'd need visas to go to Prague. "It says we can go for business or pleasure from the U.S. for up to ninety days without a visa," Sarah relayed.

"That's good news. Is your passport up to date and not expiring early next year?"

Sarah's brows furrowed. "It should be. I renewed it maybe four years ago, or maybe it was three. It was before I visited my brother in Scotland."

"You should be good then."

The waitress arrived with the fried squid, the last of their ordered dishes. "Would you like burnt Basque cheesecake, flan, or poached pears with cinnamon and vanilla for dessert?"

"Give us a few minutes, please," Sarah said. "I need to see how much room I have after this squid."

As she was leaving, Cal appeared before them and he had his mom by her wrist like he had dragged her to their table. Trish's eyes flickered with silent apology, a mix of embarrassment and pleading for understanding. She offered a tight smile, the kind that said *he doesn't mean any harm* without uttering a word. "Jared, thanks for inviting me to game. If you put your phone near mine, I can beam you my number."

"Okay. I'll be in touch by the middle of next week." Jared put his phone on the table next to where Callendale had placed his. "Or, we may see you at the fireworks. You gonna be there?"

Cal looked over his shoulder at his mother and then back at Jared. "Yeah, man. If you're going I will."

Trish silently mouthed, "Thank you," to Sarah and Jared.

"Then we'll see you there. You'll be able to find us because a red heeler cattle dog will be with us. Whiskey's the only cattle dog in Cottageville."

"Whiskey! Such a rad name." Cal's wide eyed enthusiasm made Sarah smile.

"He's a rad dog, too," Trish said.

"Aww, mom. Don't use words like rad," Cal grumbled.

"Let's let them enjoy their date." Trish put her arm on his

shoulder, steering him away from their table. "Good night, Sarah. Good night, Jared. Thank you," she said before they parted.

"Looks like Callendale McGowan…or whatever his last name is…may be the self-appointed chair of the Jared Greene fan club," Sarah teased.

"At least at whatever posh private school he goes to." Jared chuckled. "Man, this squid is so tender and sweet."

"Those were basically Em's words, too. She's the one who reminded me about this place."

After Jared placed another piece of squid in his mouth and chewed thoughtfully, he asked, "Have you learned anything new about Micas Brighton or figured out why someone would want to kill him?"

Sarah shook her head no. "I promised John I wouldn't investigate it much."

"And you're actually honoring that?" One side of Jared's mouth quirked up.

"Mostly. He intimated it could have been a professional hit and doesn't want me dead."

"I don't want you dead, either." Jared reached across their small table and put his hand on hers. "And that reminds me. We should probably make some wills, now that my art is taking off…and well, you, you own a house and have Whiskey and your business, so you should probably designate who takes care of those things."

"Interesting segue, but I agree. I'll call Moose McCabe after the holiday." Moose was the local lawyer everyone went to for wills, power of attorneys, trusts, business contracts, and anything else they thought they needed a lawyer for. Jared had paid him to review his publishing contracts, and Sarah had solicited advice from him when her business hired its first employee.

"How'd your breakfast go with Lottie? Did you find out anything that has you believing Micas' death is connected to organized crime?"

"Not really," Sarah admitted. "She did say sometimes when he was asked to authenticate a piece of art, he had to be the bearer of bad news."

"And that could piss people off," Jared finished her sentence.

"Yes." Sarah finished the sangria that was in her glass. She felt full up to her throat, but the food had been so good it was well worth a bit of overeating discomfort.

Jared ate the last two bites of torta that had been on his plate. "Did she say what he was working on the last few months?"

Sarah filled him in on the book on Grant Wood and what little she knew.

"So when we go help her clean out the house tomorrow, am I to be on the lookout for anything in particular, my favorite dog groomer-sleuth?" Jared grinned at her.

"I hate to say we'll know it when we see it...and I'm hoping that we will."

"But that's not much to go on." Jared laughed. "I'm stuffed. Let's have her box the burnt Basque cheese and take it home."

"Sounds good, but let's see if they will sell a whole cheesecake. After all, you invited Lottie for dinner tomorrow night and I told Em and Taylor they could come, too. Not sure what you had planned but that could end the meal."

"That's a solid plan. I figured I'd throw chicken breasts and a few cans of jalapenos and some other things in the slow cooker for the day. We can make tacos or Tex-Mex salads or whatever with it. We have plenty of cans of beans and shredded cheese, salsa, sour cream, and chips." Jared signaled the waitress with a curve and wiggle of his index finger.

"My head says it will be delicious, but my belly right now is groaning in protest at the concept of more food."

"I hear you."

When the waitress arrived, he asked about buying a whole cheesecake, and then he requested boxes for the rest of the food on their table and the check.

CHAPTER 19

At their usual time the next morning, Whiskey and Sarah, who had already showered and was wearing a well-worn gray t-shirt with a black drawing of a cattle dog's head over the stacked words "Every snack you make / Every meal you bake / Every bite you take / I'll be watching you" with old jeans and sneakers, walked through the park at a fast clip. Only once or twice did Whiskey stop to pee on something or sniff.

As they approached the place where the path through the park curved and where Sarah could view the playground ahead, maybe one hundred yards off to the right and the ball field the same distance away on the left, Sarah noticed someone near the swingset. The person's back was to Sarah and Whiskey. Their hands were up above their shoulders and they were fiddling with one of the chains on one swing.

Sarah stopped in her tracks. She whispered, "Heel," to Whiskey, and he parked his butt right where he was. His eyes, too, were ahead, looking at the person, who wore a black t-shirt and jeans over a narrow frame.

Sarah stood as still as a mountain, She wanted to observe without drawing attention to herself or to her dog. She wasn't sure what she was witnessing, but something felt off. Especially since the playground was most often empty at six-thirty a.m. on a Saturday.

Whatever the person was doing to the chain, they seemed to be very focused on it, fiddling with it with their fingers. They gave a tug, and then dropped their hands to the side.

Without looking around, they took off at a jog and picked up the path heading toward Main Street.

Sarah waited a beat and then she whispered, "Come on, Whisk. Let's go see the swing." And they ran to the furthest swing on the left.

As they approached Sarah noticed something small tied to the chain, and when she got within touching distance, she saw it was a pair of gold hoop earrings tied to the chain with a piece of string.

Her eyes scanned the park path for the person who had tied them to swing, but they were gone.

She pulled out her phone, searched her contacts, and called Chief James. She was sure these earrings were a part of the items stolen, most likely the earrings Rebecca Davis said were taken. And best—and worst—of all, she recognized the person who tied them to the chain.

"Good morning, Sarah," he answered, but sounded a bit groggy.

"Whiskey and I are in the park. We spied someone at the swingsets acting suspiciously, so we hung back and watched. And then came to investigate after the person left. Were the earrings Rebecca Davis had stolen a pair of gold hoops?"

"Yes."

"They are tied to a swing. And I know who tied them there, but I'd rather tell you in person."

The Chief's sigh came through the phone loudly and clearly. "That bad, huh?"

"Let's just say it will be devastating news for someone we care about."

"I'll be there in five minutes. John's on duty. I'll let him know, too."

"Umm, Chief, with all due respect, you may want to handle this yourself first."

The silence that came was almost deafening. And Sarah's first instinct was to fill it. But she reminded herself to keep quiet.

"All right, Sarah. Stay right there and don't touch anything. I'm on my way." Chief James disconnected.

Sarah decided that the best thing to do while she waited was to search the playground in case Daphne's shoes or anything else had been hidden on the slide, the jungle gym, in the sandbox, or under the seesaws. "Come on, Whiskey," she said as she walked toward the slides and crouched down to look at their undersides. Whiskey slurped the side of her face with his big pink tongue when she got down to his level.

She laughed and said, "Silly boy."

She inspected the perimeter and under the jungle gym and then each of the hollow metal bars that formed its hive-like structure. No jewelry was attached to it. And the only thing she found near it was one toddler-size Reebok. She chuckled to herself that small children always seemed to be down a sock or shoe without their parents noticing.

Sarah was searching around and under the seesaws when she saw Chief James coming up the path from the parking lot. Whiskey raced to greet him, and the Chief rewarded him by scratching under his chin.

"Find anything else?" he asked.

Sarah shook her head and her ponytail bounced.

"Show me what you've got."

She led him to the far left swing and pointed at the earrings tied to the silver link chain.

"They certainly fit the description Rebecca gave of her earrings. Gold hollow hoops, about one inch in diameter. The post clicks into a two-prong notch."

Sarah leaned closer to them to check out the closing mechanism. "That's these."

Chief James took some photos with his phone. "Now, Sarah, you want to tell me why you didn't want me to call John Beams to meet us here."

Sarah looked down at her feet and shuffled one foot and then the other. Then she raised her eyes and met his. "Because the person I saw tie these earrings to the swing was probably the person who robbed the houses."

"Most likely," Chief James agreed. "And?"

"It was Mayor Trish's son, Callendale." Sarah's mouth turned down, mimicking the way it felt like her heart had dropped, having to admit that.

Chief James whistled. "Your hesitation makes sense. But a crime is still a crime. I appreciate you calling me, Sarah. I'll take it from here. You and Whiskey can be on your way."

So many questions swirled through Sarah's head, like tumbleweeds in a tornado. But she bit her tongue, knowing it wasn't her place to ask how this would be handled or what would happen. "Okay," she said. "Come on, Whisk, let's go home."

"And Sarah?" Chief James said to her back as she took the first few tentative steps toward their house.

"Let's just keep this between you and me."

She looked over her shoulder at him. "Okay." But she really wanted to talk to Jared about it. She needed to bounce the ideas she had about why Cal would have done something like this off of someone. And she regretted not counting the money that had been sent to her with the gun. Had it all been returned? If it hadn't been, she hoped Cottageville P.D. knew she wouldn't have kept any of it. *And gosh, how was Mayor Trish going to deal with knowing her son did this? Did he do it because he was the mayor's son and thought he'd get away with it?*

When Sarah opened the front door, Jared said, "Hey, I was wondering if I needed to send a search party."

"Very funny," she said. "But you know Whisk. Sometimes he needs to sniff every little thing and leave gallons of pee-mail for his adoring fans." Sarah chuckled, but it seemed forced to her own ears.

She hoped Jared didn't notice.

He bent his head and kissed her. "Need more coffee? There's a half-pot left. And I was thinking of making us a bigger breakfast to fuel the hard work of cleaning out the house. Eggs, bacon, and hashbrowns?"

"Sounds good. I'll cut some fruit. The honeydew seems to be ripe enough now."

Sarah fed Whiskey before she started cutting and cleaning the melon. She plopped a piece in his bowl, and he gobbled it like it was the perfect dessert and then sat on his butt and pawed her leg, letting her know he wanted more. "One more, but that's all. Too much fruit and you get the runs. Don't you remember the last time?" she asked him.

At eight-fifteen, Sarah received a text from Lottie that said, "I got the keys from the police. Headed to my dad's now. Can you meet me soon?"

"Yes. We'll pack up now."

Sarah grabbed her backpack and shoved a box of black garbage bags and her thick rubber gloves into it. Jared put some basic tools in a duffle bag and a few pairs of gloves. "You taking your laptop?" he asked when he saw her backpack.

"It's in there just because I didn't remove it. And I brought some kibble and a water bowl for Whiskey."

"He's coming with us?" Jared's one eyebrow was raised.

"Yes, because it may be a long day. He'll stay out of the way. You know he will."

As they left, Jared locked up and set the alarm. Sarah opened the door for Whiskey to climb into the Jeep and she put her backpack and Jared's duffle into the back. The drive to the outskirts of town took eighteen minutes.

Micas Brighton's two-story farmhouse was white with black shutters and three gables framing double windows. The roof was green metal and cement stairs led to the white front door. The house seemed to be in good repair for its age, which Sarah estimated could be one hundred, but her first thought on seeing it was identical to Jared's comment when they pulled up in front of it. "For a man who spent his whole life with art, this house is boring."

Sarah chuckled. "Uninspired architecture. It's a rectangle with three gables, and what looks like a later addition to create an attached garage."

The front door flew open and Lottie stuck her head out saying, "Come in, come in." Her face was pale but her eyes were bright. She wore a t-shirt emblazoned with a couture company's name across her chest, straight legged jeans, and red ballet flats.

Not exactly getting dirty clothes, Sarah thought. *But maybe it was all she had with her.* "Where would you like us to start?" Sarah asked.

Whiskey pushed his way into the house and started sniffing around.

"Let me show you around first," Lottie said. "Then we'll do the assignments. I'm so grateful you are willing to help."

"Em will be here soon. Her boyfriend had to work today."

They entered a living room that had so much more character than the house's exterior. A riverstone fireplace was the focal point of one wall and artwork was displayed around the room as if it were a gallery. A metal sculpture flowing with movement and grace adorned a pedestal with built in LED lighting in one corner of the room. A breathtaking coffee table of what Sarah wasn't sure was two pieces of wood or one piece fluidly carved to look like two at a right angle and topped with a rounded triangular piece of glass which had the place of honor next to a modern, low profile leather sofa.

"Wow. A Noguchi," Jared said, reverently running his finger along the walnut base.

"One of my father's favorites," Lottie said, tears welling in her eyes.

Sarah looked at other things in the room. Paintings and etchings on the walls, all with their own lighting. Ceramics and another two sculptures on pedestals or occasional tables.

"You're taking all of these things with you, right?" Jared asked, his voice oozing with awe.

"Yes, I'll move them all to L.A. There's a Picasso ceramic somewhere here that I may auction. We'll see. If you follow me, I'll show you the rest of the place."

In the kitchen, Sarah noticed some reddish-brown stains of dried blood on the floor, and made a mental note to keep Em out of there until it was cleaned thoroughly. The kitchen was mostly practical and somewhat uninspired, with dated wooden cabinets, updated granite countertops, and stainless steel appliances. It lacked the artistry and panache that defined the living and dining rooms.

At the top of the wood staircase, Lottie showed them three bedrooms with wainscotting and white framing around doors and the windows, and two updated bathrooms. All of the rooms had art on every wall. The spare bedrooms had paintings stacked like dominoes between the bed and wall and in the closets. "He didn't have room to display it all," Lottie explained.

"He could have opened a gallery space," Jared said. "This is amazing." He gingerly moved some of the stacked paintings to see what was on the canvases. "They should really each be in a separate art box for shipping."

"Yes, I have some on order," Lottie explained. "The closest moving equipment company didn't have those in stock."

From downstairs, they heard a "Woohoo, I'm here," and Whiskey took off to acknowledge Emily's arrival.

"Up here," Sarah called from the top of the stairs.

Whiskey and Emily came up the stairs together. Em's hair was again braided and red, white, and blue, but she had replaced her combat boots with black Chuck Taylors, and wore a black The Kinks vintage t-shirt with frayed jeans shorts. Sarah hugged her assistant and said, "Glad you could make it." Then she led her into Micas Brighton's bedroom, which is where Jared and Lottie stood inside the closet, looking at all of the clothes and a few pairs of shoes.

"Lottie, this is my assistant Emily Colt. Emily, this is Carlotta Brighton."

They shook hands and exchanged "pleased to meet yous".

Jared said, "Lottie and I were discussing that all of this should be gone through to make sure there's no money or notes or anything in the pockets of the clothes, but that they need to be bagged up. The Presbyterian church said they'd take it for their clothing bank."

"That's great," Sarah said. She touched the sleeve of a couple of tweed jackets and then turned back into the room. "And in the

Chippendale wardrobe?"

"Probably my dad's undershirts and boxers and cufflinks and things. He's moved that heavy thing everywhere he's lived. It's what I always imagined I'd find the lion and the witch when I was a kid, so I never had much interest in it." Lottie smirked.

"I was more of a *Misty of Chincoteague* fan myself," Sarah said. She stepped toward the bed onto the Persian rug and pulled up the coverings, wanting to see if there were drawers under the mattress. Under her foot under the rug, Sarah felt a bit of a lump and that piqued her curiosity. She stepped back off the rug onto the hardwoods and picked up the heavy wool edge.

"Did you find the safe?" Lottie asked.

"What?" Sarah asked.

"The safe. My father always has one."

And sure enough when Sarah and Jared together lifted the carpet, they spied metal apparently held to the subflooring with anchor bolts or lag screws. "We need to move the bed over to get to it," Jared said. He dropped the rug and moved to the far side of the bed. "Everyone, grab a corner, but grab it low so we don't break posts."

He waited for Em, Lottie, and Sarah to get ahold of their part of the bedframe and then he said, "On a count of three, move it toward me and Sarah. We need to move it about a foot and a half. One, two, three."

They worked as a unit and walked to bed toward the windows overlooking the front yard. And then when it was moved, Jared and Lottie rolled the carpet toward the bed and uncovered a rectangular safe with more than a six-inch perimeter of metal framing it into the hardwood floor. "Wow," Jared said. "Must have a lot of reinforcement in the floor to hold this thing up."

"My dad does this in every house he owns. Sometimes it's in the garage, sometimes in a closet, but it is always in the floor. He thinks they are safer than the ones in the walls behind artwork." She shakes her head.

"Do you know the combination?" Sarah asked, wondering if anything in there could provide answers about his murder.

"Yes." Lottie knelt next to the safe and started spinning the dial. "It's either my birthday or my mom's. Every time."

Her first guess was right, as she tugged the heavy door open, and they all leaned over to peer inside.

CHAPTER 20

On top of what looked like a stack of files and papers were two portable hard drives. Lottie reached in and pulled those out and started handing everything in the safe to the three people around her. "Anybody have a computer with them?" she asked.

"I do," Sarah said, taking the hard drives from Emily.

"Good. Can you get your computer set up in the dining room and I'll come down in a minute and look at these drives with you?"

"Sure thing."

"Emily and Jared, can you start on my dad's clothes? Some boxes are in my rental car out front and I saw garbage bags under the kitchen sink."

Lottie scooped up the file folders, binders, and papers from the safe and carried them out of the room with her, following Sarah and Whiskey down the staircase.

Sarah grabbed her laptop by the front door and when she came into the dining room, she noticed Lottie had put two glasses of water on the table.

"I wasn't sure if you were thirsty," Lottie said.

"Thank you." She took a sip to be polite and then opened her laptop and attached the portable drive to the back of it and booted the computer. While they waited for the processor to do its start-up stuff, Sarah asked, "Do you know if your dad uses these for his research or authentication or what?"

"When I was younger, he kept literal paper trails of his research and authentication and assessments. Even when he switched to logging everything in the computer, he often kept paper copies, not trusting the computer or server or whatever to not lose his data. But I thought with the cloud, he started storing everything digitally..." Her voice trailed off and she frowned.

Sarah said, "But maybe he's doing both or these are his backups of what is in the cloud?" Her eyebrows raised in question.

"Maybe. I guess we'll find out soon enough." She pointed at Sarah's screen where a photo of a younger Whiskey with his eyes happy, his tongue hanging low, and his fur wet from a swim suddenly appeared.

"What a fun photo. He's such a lovely dog," Lottie said.

Sarah used her touchpad to click on the icon for the removable drive. The drive made a soft whirring noise before a narrow rectangle appeared on Sarah's screen, asking for a password. She looked at Lottie for the answer.

Wrinkles formed on Lottie's forehead. "Umm, try Matisse1954."

"Access denied."

"Matisse1131954."

"Access denied. And I'm not sure how many tries we get." Sarah eyed the stack of folders Lottie had placed on the table. Some had dates on the tab, written European style. One said 24 June 1995. "Hey, Lottie. What are the numbers with the word Matisse?"

"When he died."

"So he died in 1954. What month and day?"

"November 3. His work and life was the subject of my dad's master's thesis and his doctoral dissertation."

Sarah could hear Jared and Emily moving about in the room overhead. Their voices were muffled. She keyed in "Matisse3111954," and hoped the M was capitalized.

The disk drive started humming and file names started listing on her screen. "Which should we open first?"

"Let's start with the most recent." Lottie pointed to it with one well-shaped unpainted nail.

The file was titled, "Maslow02062025". Sarah pointed the cursor to the file and hit enter. A word document opened with all of the details about two landscape paintings that were allegedly by Grant Wood. Micas Brighton had recorded their dimensions, included photos, and made meticulous notes. His analysis ran for a number of pages that Sarah carefully read.

When she got to the last sentence on the last page, Sarah eyed

Lottie, trying to gauge her emotional state. Lottie's eyes didn't leave the screen. So Sarah quietly stated, "Your dad found the paintings to be excellent forgeries, but forgeries nonetheless. And his notes say Peter Maslow did not respond well to that and Peter asked him to lie in his report."

"My father would never do that," Lottie insisted, her eyes turning glossy. She stood and walked from the table to the windows and looked out across the yard. Her arms were crossed over her chest, like she was trying to comfort herself.

Sarah debated going to stand with her but felt like maybe Lottie needed a minute. She read through the file list while she waited and clicked open another file with the Maslow name and another date. She skimmed that one and found that the small statue in question had indeed been authentic. Another similar file on an antique vase said the same thing: the piece was made by the suspected artist.

Sarah glanced up from the computer and realized Lottie had turned around and was looking toward her, though Sarah wasn't sure if Lottie was seeing her. Pain flashed through Lottie's eyes like lightning in a dark sky. "Do you think his refusal got him killed?"

"It may have." Sarah's voice was soft.

Lottie shivered though the room was rather warm. "By the Maslows?" she whispered.

"I'm not sure," Sarah said. "I think we need to read through the report again to see if there is mention of the paintings' provenance or if anyone's names are here besides the Maslows. Do you want to do that with me?" Sarah patted the chair next to hers.

"Yes. No. Maybe." Lottie grimaced. "I'm having trouble

wrapping my head around the idea that people my father worked with and liked could have done this. And they've been so nice to me."

Sarah thought Glenda was nice. Peter she wasn't so sure about, but she really didn't know him or either of them. *Could he have gambled too much and gotten into debt with the wrong people? Is that why he needed the paintings to be the works of Grant Wood? Even nice people sometimes did horrible things, when they were desperate, scared, or felt they had no other choice. But then again, they were victims, too. Their business was broken into...*

Sarah realized Lottie was watching her. "Your face has said so many things."

Sarah flashed her a slip of a smile. "I was trying to reason it out. The break-in at the antique store, what happened to your father, his report about the paintings and his note about Peter's reaction and request."

"Did you come to any conclusions?"

"I've mostly come to more questions."

Lottie waved a finger at Sarah's computer. "Let's read that report one more time and look at the other files to see what's there. Then we'll flip through this pile of papers."

"Okay," Sarah said. "And then we can start cleaning the kitchen and packing things up. Sometimes repetitive or mindless actions jar a piece of the mental puzzle loose."

"You mean like how the best ideas come while taking a shower?" Lottie asked.

"Exactly." Sarah grinned at her, and then started reading what was on her screen.

Six minutes later they were done re-reading the report. Sarah brought up the file list again and explained to Lottie that she had looked at the other files for the Maslows, mostly based on curiosity to see whether other pieces of art had been authenticated. They skimmed through a few more recent files but nothing stood out to them.

"Let's check the other portable drive," Lottie said.

Sarah closed out of the one drive and disconnected it and then plugged the second drive into the port at the back of her laptop. The request for a password popped up, and Sarah tried the same password as the last time. Access was granted, and the file names cascaded onto her screen like a waterfall.

"For a guy who puts a safe in his floor, he didn't secure his electronic files very well, using the same password over and over."

"That's true," Lottie admitted. "I just hope he chose something different for his bank accounts."

The files on the second drive seemed much the same as the first though was one labeled "Grant Wood Book" and others referenced various papers that Sarah remembered seeing during her Micas Brighton web search. A half an hour later, they were reviewing the stack of documents and making piles: legal, personal, academic. Jared and Emily came down the stairs, with Whiskey hot on their heels.

"How's it going?" Jared asked.

Sarah and Lottie filled them in, and then Lottie asked, "Find anything interesting in the clothes?"

"Cash, coins, old receipts," Jared said. "I started piles for each at the base of the Chippendale armoire, after we cleaned it out. Some of the underwear was old, same with the socks. Some had holes. We pitched those. I hope that's okay."

Lottie smiled. "Fine by me. I'm even grateful."

"How much cash did you find? And what were the receipts from?" Sarah's curiosity went into overdrive.

"A few hundred dollars?" Jared raised his eyes at Emily for confirmation.

"Yeah, we didn't count it, but it was way more than you'd find hidden in my clothes." Emily giggled.

"The receipts were from local stores and restaurants. A dozen or more were lottery tickets—"

Before he could say more Lottie cut in, "My dad didn't play the lottery. He called it a 'fool's game' and said odds were better at Vegas, which he disdained. His brother lost his life to a gambling addiction."

Sarah's eyes were wide, and she pointedly looked from Jared to her assistant. "Were the lottery tickets all together or were they spread out in multiple items of clothing?"

"I found them, Sarah," Em said. "They were in the pocket of one pair of pants, folded together. I thought it was weird so I looked at them closely. The tickets had a bunch of different dates on them from the last six months. The ticket costs were high, not like the dollar or two someone spends on the Powerball. And I'm not sure they were state lottery anyway. His other pocket on the same pants had four fifty dollar scratcher tickets. None were winners."

"Were there any receipts in that same pair of pants?" Sarah asked, trying to determine when those pants were last worn.

Emily's face squinched like she was thinking hard and then it lit up and her eyes opened like an anime character's. "Yes. One receipt from the Italian restaurant next to the Coiffure." She raced out of the room, and Sarah heard her run up the stairs. Whiskey gave chase like it was a game.

When they returned to the dining room, Emily's energy vibrated like a hummingbird. Talking so fast she ran the words together, she said, "Sarah, the date on the receipt is last Saturday night. The night of the robberies. And if these lottery tickets weren't Micas Brighton's, they could be Mr. Maslow's. Maybe Micas found them at the antique store and...and...but why would he take them?" Emily ran out of steam and confusion was written on her countenance.

"Maybe because he thought it explained why Peter Maslow was pressuring him to authenticate two forgeries," Sarah said. Her voice was level and emotionless. "Lottie, you said your dad understood from personal experience the pain that a gambling addiction can cause in a family. I want to look at those tickets and see what the total spent on them was. If someone is buying fifty dollar or more lottery tickets on the regular, that screams desperation to me. And desperate people sometimes do horrendous things."

Jared said, "I agree. But what about the break-in to the antique store? The Maslows didn't break their own window. They weren't even in the state."

Sarah let loose a sigh and then took a big inhale. She knew she could trust Em and Jared, and she made a split second decision to trust Lottie. "I need the three of you to promise not to tell anyone what I'm about to tell you. Chief James asked me to hold my tongue, but I need your brain power. Whoever broke into the antique store stole two paintings that Micas Brighton had been hired to authenticate...

and Lottie and I have discovered on this portable hard drive that they were both well done forgeries and that Peter Maslow was pissed about it. The other things taken from the antique store were their computer and portable hard drives, plus their safe was removed from the wall and drilled."

"Holy cow," Emily said. "That's way different than the other burglaries."

At the same time Jared said, "Doing that makes a lot of noise."

"Exactly. And most of the town was at the movie in the park. I believe the break in at the antique store was done by professionals. Maybe mob related. Maybe a loan shark Peter owed a gambling debt. Or maybe someone who wanted access to the report for the paintings so that they could doctor them in their favor. I'm unsure of it, but I'd stake my reputation as Sarahlock Holmes, as Candace Grimes called me—" Sarah smirked—"that the antique store and its theft is connected to the shooting of Lottie's father and that neither is connected to the other burglaries."

Jared said, "How long have you known the details of the antique store burglary?"

"Since I went to see Mrs. Maslow. Officer Beams said the information I learned wasn't released to the public so he asked for my discretion. Lottie, if your father suspected Peter Maslow had a gambling problem, would he have talked to him about it?"

"He considered them friends, so yeah, probably."

Something occurred to Sarah. Something bothered her about the gun being left here in the house at the scene of the crime. She asked Lottie, "Did your dad own a gun?"

"He abhorred them. Almost as much as gambling." She flattened her lips and her eyes filled with unshed tears. So quietly that Sarah almost didn't hear her, Lottie said, "It's how my uncle died."

Sarah's heart felt like it seized. *Her uncle and her father both died by gunshot?* She put her hand on Lottie's. "I'm so sorry," Sarah said, meaning the words and sentiment deeply.

Lottie's tears fell. "Thank you, guys, for caring for me, a stranger." Her eyes met each of theirs in turn. When her eyes got to Emily's, Em said, "It's what we do. I've lived here all of my life and people take care of each other. What do you need us to do next?"

Jared said, "Hang on a second, Em. If what Sarah thinks is right, that Micas' declaration of the paintings being fakes is at the heart of these crimes, then we need to figure out if there's enough evidence to call Chief James."

"I don't think there is, Jared. Right now it is mostly speculation," Sarah said.

"But what if we could get more proof? Yesterday...or was it on Thursday, we talked about the illegal gambling that goes on in the back room of Butch's Brewery. Maybe someone who's a regular can tell us if Peter Maslow is too, and if he usually wins or loses."

Emily jumped in with, "Me. I can find that out. Like I said, my dad's best friend goes there. He'd know. They are on the golf course right now. Let me go ask them."

"How will you do that without telling him why?" Sarah asked.

"Umm," Emily stalled, and then a gleam appeared in her eye. "Can I tell a white lie?"

Sarah gave her a 'what you talking about' look, that caused

Emily to giggle.

"I'll tell them that now that Jared is semi-famous and making some bank, that he wants to join the game and so I'll ask my dad's friend if he can make the introductions…or something like that. I'll figure it out on the drive over there."

"Won't they think it's weird that you show up on the golf course to ask that question?" Sarah asked. "I think a phone call could handle it."

"But I want to see their faces. But point taken, I'll video call." Emily pulled her phone from her back pocket and walked from the dining room into the living room. Whiskey watched her go, but decided not to get up from where he was curled on the floor.

"Anyone want anything?" Lottie asked. "I brought some soft drinks with me, but I saw that my dad has coffee and tea. And there's enough stuff in the fridge that I can make sandwiches."

"I'd drink some coffee," Jared said, "but let me help you with that."

He shot a look at Sarah that she read as he didn't want Lottie to be alone in the kitchen where her father died. "I'll come too and start to clean the place." She left her laptop, the drives, and the files on the dining room table.

Sarah found a mop and a bucket in a utility area by the back door. She filled it with water and threw in some full caps of bleach. The floor was old linoleum that had once been white so she figured the bleach would do nothing but improve its state. She waited for Lottie to make the sandwiches and Jared the coffee before she got to work. Lottie explained, "My dad wasn't much of a cook, so the kitchen was the last on his list of home improvements." She and Jared took the food and beverages back to the dining room.

Sarah donned her rubber gloves and used granite cleaner on the counters, diluted Murphy's oil soap on all of the cabinets, and then the bucket of bleach water and mop on the floor. At one point, Whiskey stuck his head around the counter, sneezed because of the stench of the bleach, and backed out of the room. "Stay away from here, dog. For your own health."

When everything was sparkling and blood-free, Sarah dumped the old water in the utility sink and hung her gloves over the side of the basin to dry. She followed the sound of voices into the dining room and picked up her glass of water and drained it. Jared held out a plate with a sandwich.

Sarah noticed the artwork had been stripped from the walls and was now stacked atop a sideboard.

"What'd I miss?" she asked.

Emily said, "Pete was a regular at poker night and a regular loser. He's been banned from the games because he owes too many people too much."

"How much is too much?" Sarah asked.

"I didn't want to ask. But my dad's BFF said that the poker players questioned if Pete didn't have his own place robbed for the insurance money. Said they think he's in dire straits. Isn't that a band?" Em flashed Sarah a lopsided grin.

Jared answered, "It is. But it also means he's screwed."

"So what you're saying is that if I decide to sell anything in this house, I probably don't want to sell it through the Maslows?" Lottie asked.

Sarah's head swiveled so fast toward her new friend she almost got whiplash. She caught the quirk of Lottie's lip and realized she was being sarcastic. "Funny," Sarah said, "and to misquote Shakespeare, something's funny in the town of Cottageville." She ate two more bites of her sandwich and then said, "Wait. Glenda Maslow told me they had just gotten the paintings in and didn't even have time to photograph them. And yet your dad's report contains photos of the two paintings. Then again, Glenda also said the artist was someone other than Grant Wood. If Glenda is claiming they don't have photos, maybe they didn't give them to the police either. That could be the reason for me to call Chief James and then I can work in some of the other information we found." Sarah reached for her phone, which she had placed next to her computer. Before she dialed she looked from Jared to Emily to Lottie to see if anyone had any objections.

"It's the best we've got," Jared said.

CHAPTER 21

Two hours later, after Sarah had been through her hypothesis with Officer John Beams three times and Jared, Emily, and Lottie had chimed in at the appropriate times, John said goodbye taking the two portable hard drives and the lottery tickets in evidence bags with him. Emily had taken boxes into one of the spare bedrooms and was going through books on shelves page by page in case any notes or money or anything useful was hidden within them. The paperbacks she put in one box so Lottie could take them to the used bookstore. The hardbacks she put in another just in case Lottie wanted to keep them.

Sarah was in a second bedroom doing something similar with

Whiskey supervising, while Jared and Lottie were going through the tools and equipment in the attached garage. Sarah said loud enough for Emily to hear her next door, "Maybe we should encourage Lottie to have an estate or garage or yard sale. There's so much stuff here that people could use. It seems a shame to dump it all at a thrift store or wherever."

"I agree," Em shouted back. "I'd buy some of these books off her."

"Set them aside and ask her," Sarah said. She put her arms over her head and stretched. All of the scrubbing and moving the bed and now sitting with her head hanging down over the books was making her stiff. She decided to do one more shelf and then take a break.

Emily's voice suddenly broke through the quiet. "Hey, Sarah, did you know Mayor Trish has a son?"

"I met him last night at the tapas restaurant," Sarah said.

"Well the message board just sent an alert. Chief James was seen earlier today leading him out of his mother's house in handcuffs. There's a photo. How old is he?"

"Fifteen. And that's a shame. People shouldn't post the sad plight of others." Sarah kept her eyes focused on the book in front of her. Part of her felt reassured that justice and punishment was blind to lineage in their town. The other part of her felt devastated for Trish. And it was that part that put the tears in her eyes.

"Sarah." Em stood in the doorway of the guest room. Their eyes met. "You don't seem surprised. Someone posted that he's been charged with breaking and entering those four houses." She paused for fifteen seconds and when Sarah said nothing, she asked, "When did you know?"

"This morning." Sarah's voice was low. "I saw him in the park this morning tying Rebecca Davis' earrings to a swing. He didn't see me and Whisk and I didn't know what exactly he was doing until I checked it out after he left. And then I called the Chief. He asked me not to tell anyone. And I didn't. Not even J." A single tear fell from Sarah's right eye.

"Aww. Sarah. That sucks." Emily sat on the floor in front of her.

"He was so excited to meet Jared. Turns out he's a big fan. Trish said he goes to boarding school and usually lives on breaks with his dad but his dad just got married to a twenty-three year old and is taking a three-month honeymoon. So Cal was sent here for the summer. Here where he has no friends and where there's not much for him to do, at least not like he's used to in New York City."

"From the city that never sleeps to the place that is mostly asleep," Emily joked. "It's rough. I wonder if this will screw up his future."

"It will be interesting to see how it plays out."

"So one mystery you solved, Sarah, and maybe the second and third mystery, too."

"I'm not sure about that, Emily. My guess is still that a professional thug broke into the antique store, but I'm not sure who came into this house and killed Micas Brighton. But I do feel strongly it had to do with those paintings."

"Were the Maslows back in town when Micas died?"

"I think so. They either got back on Sunday or early Monday morning, but I'm not sure what time the police determined Micas was shot."

"We should have asked Officer Beams while he was here."

"Yes, that would have been a good idea. But he also asked me to stay out of investigating this crime, and so far, I've kept my promise. At least until we found the safe."

"Why's that, Sarah?"

"Why'd he ask me to stay out of it? Because they think it is a professional hit and John said he didn't want to see me dead."

"I don't either." Emily patted Sarah's leg. "I don't want to wash all of those dogs by myself." She grinned.

"I wouldn't wish that on you either. Did you finish the books in your room?"

"I did. Want me to help you finish yours?"

"That'd be nice."

They worked together side by side, occasionally commenting on a book or a fun bookmark that was stuck inside a tome. Some had quotes of famous authors, some were embossed leather, and some were thin metal like an old-school ruler. Emily started a separate pile of them and thought maybe Lottie should sell them on Etsy or eBay or somewhere.

Once the books were done in all three bedrooms, Whiskey, Sarah, and Emily went back downstairs. It was now late afternoon, and Sarah was getting hungry. She popped her head into the garage and saw Jared and Lottie hard at work sorting tools onto a table from a standing tool chest that was almost as tall as Jared. "Hey, how about we call it a day and go to our house and eat? Lottie, if you want, you can stay over. We have a guest room with its own ensuite bathroom." Sarah wanted to make sure Lottie knew she didn't have to stay here in this house.

"That's sweet. But I'll probably just head back to the inn. We can stop now and start again tomorrow."

"Maybe you should think of having a yard or estate sale for furniture you don't want, the tools and equipment, things like that," Sarah said.

"We can help," Emily piped up.

"You guys are so nice. I'm not sure how I could have gotten through this without you." Lottie wiped her hands on a rag on the table and then walked to Sarah and Em. "May I follow you to the house?"

"Yes, but let me give you our address, just in case we get separated." Sarah held out her hand for Lottie's phone. Then she packed up her laptop and they double checked every window and exterior door of the house was locked and formed a caravan down the driveway with Sarah's green CJ leading the way. But they got as far as the north end of Main Street to find a fire engine across the road blocking any traffic and a state patrol officer standing by. Sarah rolled down her window. "What's going on?" She didn't know the state patrol officer but she waved to the firefighter whom she had seen around town.

"Main Street is closed due to a situation. You have to detour around." The officer pointed to the direction he wanted them to go.

"What kind of situation?" Sarah asked.

"Can't say. Move along." The officer pointed again.

"Yes, sir," Sarah said. She left her window down and waved her arm out the window for the two cars behind her, driven by Lottie and Emily to follow her.

"You want to poke around on your phone?" she asked Jared,

"See if the message board says anything?"

"Focus on driving," Jared mumbled, while typing his security code into his phone.

By the time they pulled into the driveway, Jared admitted, "I've got nothing. No messages. No scanner activity. No tweets from official or even unofficial channels."

"That's strange." Sarah exited the Jeep and waited for Whiskey to climb over the seat to get out before she went to the cargo area to get her backpack. "Where's your duffle?" she asked Jared.

"I left it there since we'll be back in the morning."

"Oh okay." Both Emily and Lottie had parked at the curb.

Sarah opened the front door and was quick to turn off the alarm as Whiskey barreled into the house like a curry of squirrels was on his tail seeking vengeance for all of the times he had chased them up trees. "Slow down, Whisk," Sarah commanded as the dog slid on the hardwoods into the side of the leather sofa.

The aroma of chicken and chiles filled the house, making Sarah's stomach growl in response.

"Anyone need to wash up? Want a shower?" Sarah asked her guests. "We have three bathrooms."

"I'll wash my hands," Lottie said.

"Down the hall and on the left you'll see a powder room."

Without being told where to go, Emily made her way into the guest bedroom and its bathroom. She yelled back to Sarah, "Can I use the towels in here?"

"They are clean."

Jared had gone into the kitchen and was pulling out things from the fridge: bags of lettuce, shredded cheese, sour cream, tortillas, salsa, whole tomatoes, hot sauce. "What else do we need?" he asked Sarah.

"Beans." She handed him three cans from the pantry and he chopped some onion and garlic and put it into a pan to sizzle before throwing the beans on top of it.

When Lottie appeared in the kitchen she asked, "Can I help?"

"There's not much to do," Jared said. "We have beer, wine, tequila, water, and iced tea."

"What's everyone else drinking?" Lottie asked.

Sarah said, "Jared will probably have beer. I'll open the wine. And Em will have iced tea."

"I'll have some wine with you."

Sarah grabbed the bottle and two glasses and headed to the dining room where she set the items on the table. "Take a seat. Open the wine. I'll be back. I need to feed Whiskey his supper."

The doorbell on Sarah's house chimed, which set off Whiskey's barking rant.

"I've got it," Em yelled, jogging from the guest room to the front door. "It's Travis."

Sarah grabbed another plate, napkin, and set of silverware for the table from her kitchen cabinets. When she returned to the dining room, she heard Em introduce Lottie and Travis, and then ask Travis what he wanted to drink.

"I'll get it," Sarah offered, heading back into the kitchen. She helped Jared put the food into serving bowls and she carried the beer and some of the food into the dining room before heading back to help carry more bowls.

When everyone was seated at the table and passing around food, creating salads and tacos, Jared asked, "Any rumors at the salon about what's going on on Main Street?"

"Only that the police are at the antique store. And someone said they aren't being allowed in."

Sarah's eyes widened and her heart raced like a thoroughbred at the Kentucky Derby. "There's a standoff?"

"I don't know," Travis admitted. "It's a rumor. You know how those go. Part truth. Part not so much."

"And I thought this was a sleepy little town," Lottie mumbled, taking a deep pull from her wine glass.

"Like any place, it has its secrets," Jared said.

"Yeah, like the mayor had a son no one knew about," Em said.

"Barbara and the Chief must have known. She and Trish are BFFs," Sarah said between bites of chicken. "Mmm, this is so good. Jared, you're amazing."

"It really is good," Lottie said. "Do you cook like this often?"

Sarah answered for him. "Almost every day. Aren't I the luckiest woman alive?" She grinned at her man, who reached over and squeezed her hand.

"We're both blessed," Jared said, before changing the subject to what Lottie's life was like in Los Angeles, what was new in its art scene, and if she had a significant other or pet back home waiting on her.

By the time nine rolled around, yawning had become contagious. "I'm gonna go," Em said. "What time do you want to start tomorrow?"

"Would you like my help? I'm off," Travis said.

"How about nine?" Lottie said. "We can finish boxing stuff up and organizing it in the garage. And maybe you can help me find local places to take some of the stuff and then plan an estate sale for next weekend. Does that sound good?"

"That's absolutely fine," Sarah said. "You okay to drive back to the inn? If not, you can take the guest room. The sheets are clean."

"I'm fine to drive. I appreciate your help and your hospitality."

Sarah, Jared, and Whiskey saw their friends to the door and watched them as they drove away. Jared put his arm around Sarah. "It's been a good day. I'm glad we're able to help her."

"Me too," she said on autopilot, staring into the darkness of the night.

"But something is on your mind," Jared prompted.

"I want to know what's going on at the antique store. Do you think we can cut through the park and—"

"No. We aren't going anywhere near there. Let the police do their jobs, babe. They are trained to handle whatever situation is there," Jared cut Sarah off.

"But—"

"No. No buts. We are going to bed." He shut the front door and engaged the locks and then said, "Come on, Whiskey, let's go do a last call in the back." And man and his adopted dog headed toward the back door.

Sarah padded in stocking feet into their bedroom. In her heart, she knew Jared was right. But her curiosity was niggling at her like a hangnail—small, persistent, and impossible to ignore. She audibly exhaled her frustration. Should she text Candace? But if Candace was at the scene and bad things were going down, Sarah didn't want to provide a distraction. She put her thumbnail between her front teeth and bit down. Patience really wasn't one of her virtues. But she knew she should do the adult thing and wait. She'd have the answers she sought soon enough. She brushed her teeth and got ready for bed.

Ten minutes later when Jared and Whiskey were in the bed, too, Jared's arms went around her and kissed the top of her head. "Thank you for not going to investigate tonight. I love you and prefer you being safe here with me. Whatever the Maslows have gotten involved in, whatever killed Micas is above our amateur paygrade. Let the professionals deal with it. I'm sure we'll have answers in the morning."

CHAPTER 22

Morning certainly brought answers, but they weren't anything like what Sarah expected. At six-forty-five, she, Jared, and Whiskey walked through Cottageville Park as usual. The park was deserted except for a few squirrels and some birds. Whiskey wandered this way and that, sniffing and marking his territory, leaving the canine version of personal ads. Java and Juice was closed today since it was Sunday, but Whiskey was determined to see his friend Bill, so he led his humans out of the park and up the sidewalk.

Bill sat at the table on his front porch, his paper spread in front of him and his coffee cup off to the side. His coloring was good, Sarah noted, as Whiskey bounded up the stairs and parked his butt next to

Bill's feet. The dog held up one paw as if he were saluting, though he was asking Bill to slap him five.

The almost-octogenarian laughed and put his palm against Whiskey's paw pads. Then he handed the dog a beef biscuit from the ever-present container on his table. "How are you three today?" Bill asked.

"We're good. How are you feeling?" Sarah couldn't believe it had only been a week since Bill's heart attack. So much had happened in that week, and Bill had a healthy glow about him.

His clear blue eyes sparkled as he said, "I feel fantastic. Thank you for asking."

He leaned closer to them. "We had some drama last night. Did you hear?"

"We tried to drive down Main Street only to find the road closed by a fire engine and the state police," Sarah admitted.

"I was sitting out here with Gladys and the girls when Officers Beams and Grimes showed up as the antique store was closing for the day. John went up onto the porch while Candace stayed by the car. He tried to open the door, but Glenda was on the other side of it and yelled he couldn't come in. He told her to open up, that he wanted to talk to Peter, and she screamed at him to go away. We could hear every word. Then suddenly he yells, 'She's got a gun,' and jumps over the railing of the front porch to the sidewalk and Candace crouches down behind the car."

"Holy crap," Sarah said.

"Seriously? What did she hope to accomplish, pulling a gun on the police?" Jared asked rhetorically.

"Then what happened?" Sarah asked.

"Then Officer Grimes called for backup. Beams kept yelling for Glenda to put down the weapon. That he knew she didn't want to hurt anyone. And she yelled back, 'Oh yes I do. I'm sick and tired of Peter hurting me, hurting us. He's a weak, small-minded man. He's bankrupted us and killed Micas Brighton and he deserves to die.'" Bill paused and took a sip of his coffee.

Sarah's eyes were huge. Her heart was thumping in her chest. "Peter shot Micas?"

"That's what Glenda said. She also yelled that it was the mafia he owed money to that broke into their business. That Peter was trying to sell them bogus paintings to cover his debt."

"All of this was yelled at the police? Where was Peter?" Sarah asked.

"We couldn't see from the porch. I assume he was inside. John tensed at one point at what I assume was the ratchet of a shotgun. The Maslows always kept one under their counter in case of theft. Anyway, more police arrived, and then the Parks with the ambulance just in case and the fire department. They had the place surrounded. For a while Glenda stopped talking to them. But then maybe an hour and a half or two hours after the whole thing started, Glenda yelled an expletive in the middle of 'I'll kill you.' There was one shotgun blast that sounded like it blew a glass vase apart or something. And the police busted their way into the building. The Parks took Peter away, though I saw he was also handcuffed to the gurney. And Glenda was handcuffed and put in the back of the police cruiser."

"Wow," Sarah and Jared said simultaneously, and then Sarah

asked Bill, "Did you know Peter Maslow was a gambler?"

"I knew he was banned from Butch's."

"For secret gambling, those games don't seem to be all that hidden."

Bill shrugged. "Towns like ours, some things are open secrets."

"I feel bad for Glenda," Sarah said.

"Yes, but she had choices. Brandishing a gun at law enforcement doesn't usually end well," Jared said, placing his hand on Sarah's lower back.

"I wonder if what Glenda said is true, that Peter killed Micas? If that's the case, I hope police find evidence to support that. I want justice to be served. Lottie deserves that."

"Everyone deserves that," Bill said.

"I'm glad you and Gladys and the poodles were safe in all of that drama," Sarah said, hugging Bill.

"Me too. Will you be at the fireworks Monday night? We'd like to sit with you again, and I'll try not to have a heart attack this time," Bill joked.

"That's an excellent plan," Sarah said. "We're headed back to Micas Brighton's today to help his daughter pack up his house and prepare for an estate sale next weekend."

"That place is crazy. It's so full of art. Amazing pieces. Gladys would love it," Jared said.

Bill's eyebrows raised. "Do you think Lottie would mind if Glad and I stopped by?"

"Not at all," Sarah said. "We're meeting her at nine so come any time thereafter."

Sarah, Jared, and Whiskey went back through the park on their way home. Jared held her hand, swinging their arms between them. He said, "Do you realize that stumbling across that safe and finding the hard drives is what set in motion the events at the antique store yesterday? Without you sending the police on that path, they may never have known who killed Micas Brighton and why."

"I'm not sure I'm finding comfort in that. I mean, I'm glad we are at the end of both mysteries. But the heartache that Mayor Trish must be feeling, that Lottie and Glenda are experiencing, make my emotions heavier than ten anchors."

Jared threw his free arm around her front and pulled her against his chest in the middle of the park path. "That's one of the reasons I love you, Sarah. You feel all the things. That's one thing that makes you amazing."

A couple of hours later, Whiskey, Jared, and Sarah pulled up in front of Micas Brighton's house to find Em's car already parked in the driveway with Emily inside the Honda. Sarah tapped on Em's window. "Whatcha doing?"

"Waiting. Listening to a true crime podcast. No one is here yet." Emily stepped out of the vehicle and Sarah squealed at her assistant's denim shorts overalls painted with white stars and her red tank top adding color underneath.

"Taking patriotism to a whole new level," Sarah said.

"Something like that." Emily's grin stretched across her face. The lip stain she wore matched her tank top.

A car came up the gravel driveway. Lottie said through the open window. "Sorry I'm late. The police stopped by." Her eyes were red rimmed and it was clear she had been crying.

"So you heard?" Sarah asked softly.

"Heard what?" Emily asked.

"You're usually on top of all the gossip," Sarah said, as Jared said, "That Peter Maslow killed Lottie's dad."

Lottie gave a single nod. "They said he will make a full recovery, the bastard."

"Wait, what? What'd I miss?" Emily asked, following Lottie into the house.

Sarah grabbed her assistant's arm to hold her back, while Jared and Lottie continued through the house and into the garage. Sarah called after him, "Don't forget about Bill and Gladys."

"I'll let her know," Jared said.

Sarah guided Emily into the living room and filled her in on everything Bill witnessed and overheard. Emily interjected, "No way" and "oh my" and "OMG" at various points, but when Sarah got to the end, she said, "Such a tragedy, Sarah. 'Oh what tangled webs we weave, when we first practice to deceive'."

"Sir Walter Scott, really?"

Emily shrugged. "It was the quote at the start of that mystery novel you got for me from the library. Seemed to fit."

"It did indeed."

"And now you're rhyming with it." Emily smirked. "So, what shall we clean out next? How can we best help Lottie? And what kind of car did Micas drive? Taylor's looking for a used vehicle so I said I'd check."

They walked off toward the garage and Lottie and Jared's voices, with Whiskey nipping at their heels, to create the game plan for the day.

The next day after eating way too much food and playing lawn games at Daniel and Ginger's, Jared, Sarah, Whiskey, and Lottie spread a blanket on the ground at Cottageville Park. Night was falling and stars were visible overhead. The humans laid back to view them, admire them, and wish upon them. Their moments of stillness were interrupted by the arrival of Janice, Bill, and Gladys with Kahlo and Cassatt. Lottie was thrilled with the poodles' names. She and Gladys had connected over art the day before, and Gladys had offered to be Lottie's adopted grandmother, since she was now without family.

"That would make you my sister,' Sarah said, grinning at her designer-wearing, L.A.-based counterpart.

"I've always wanted a sister," Lottie said, looping her arm through Sarah's.

Whiskey sniffed each of the poodles hello before settling back down and curling himself into a ball on the blanket. It was close to his bedtime.

Sarah glanced around the park and noticed it was filling up. Some children were in their pajamas. Others wore regular clothes but clutched stuffed animals or toys. A few were already curled with their heads on their parents' legs fast asleep.

Mayor Trish's voice came through the P.A. system and Sarah turned toward the makeshift stage. "Greetings, everyone. Happy Independence Day. As I'm sure you've heard, my son is in town and caused some stress for some of you and your households. For that I am deeply sorry." She was silent for a few beats and so were most of the people in the park.

Then she continued, "This time of year, we often talk about freedom. We are so grateful to our military personnel both past and present and for those who gave their lives for our country and for our freedoms. We are grateful to our first responders who help us in our daily lives and keep our community safe and free. But with freedom comes responsibility, as Eleanor Roosevelt wisely said. And because I need to take responsibility for what happened over the last week and for way before that, I will be taking a three-month sabbatical from being Cottageville Mayor. My father, our former mayor, will be filling in during my absence. I hope you all understand. I love being your mayor, but this will be my last public event until autumn."

Stunned silence ricocheted throughout the park, but then one person started to clap followed by another and another until everyone was on their feet clapping, supporting their leader for doing what was best for her son, herself, and their community.

"Thank you," Mayor Trish said, tears streaming down her face. "And thank you to Dazzling D fireworks for the show that's about to begin. I love you, all. Happy Independence Day."

THE END

DEADLY LIES
AND
DOG-EARED SECRETS

CHAPTER 1

The green door of Carter's Canine Coiffure opened, letting in a crisp gust of late October air scented with dry leaves and woodsmoke. Red-haired Sarah Carter, age twenty-eight, barely looked up from the Australian red heeler cattle dog in her stainless steel tub. Her hands were buried in a mountain of soap suds that clung to Whiskey's rough but soft coat like clouds around the Mt. Everest's peak.

"*Bonjour,*" Sarah called to Daphne Smith, a well-dressed and eccentric woman who spoke mostly French, though she had lived in Cottageville, Iowa, her whole life and had never traveled to Quebec, Montreal, or Paris, or anywhere where the language was native.

Daphne wore a black cashmere turtleneck sweater over burnt orange pants tucked into black riding boots. She carried her costume-wearing buff colored French bulldog Pierre, who was dressed as a bee and looking none too happy about it, under her arm like a football.

Twenty-year-old Emily Colt, Sarah's assistant groomer and close friend, stepped forward to the counter. "*Bonjour,* Daphne. *Bonjour,* Pierre. You make a cute bee." She reached out her hand and scratched between his ears.

"*Nous sommes en crise. Pierre s'est cassé un ongle. Il faut le réparer.*" Daphne used her hands to spread the toes on Pierre's front left foot. One toenail was barely hanging on. Fortunately for the dog and for Emily, it hadn't broken to the quick. And though Em didn't speak French, she understood what Daphne was showing her. One fast snip and the problem was solved.

"*Tu es une bouée de sauvetage.*" Daphne patted Emily's hand, threw a twenty on the counter, and then walked out the door.

"If it was all that easy," Emily said to Sarah.

"Well done," Sarah said, rinsing Whiskey until the water ran clear. Whiskey didn't require many baths, maybe one or two a year. Cattle dogs tended to stay clean and rarely stank. Their double coat and natural grooming abilities kept them mostly clean and dry. Case in point being how Whiskey bit his own toenails and scratched them against pavement when they needed to be trimmed or worn down. He hated Sarah to get anywhere near him with the clippers, and he had been that way since he was a pup, seven years ago.

When Sarah shut off the water, Whiskey gave a happy shake, sending droplets flying across the room. Emily squealed in delight, her rosy painted cheeks bunching toward her eyes. Emily often dressed edgy and often in black, but today she surprised Sarah by coming to work wearing a blue and white gingham pinafore over a white blouse. She had extensions in her hair that were bowed with the same blue and white gingham into two ponytails, one down each side of her face and dress front.

"Dorothy?" Sarah had asked, her eyebrows raised in surprise.

"Iconic," Em said.

Sarah planned to change into her costume when they were done with work for the day. This afternoon was the annual Halloween Pet Parade, and Sarah was so grateful the city council and mayor's office took charge of it. Sarah and Emily had already organized one Cottageville Pet Parade this year for Valentine's Day, and while it was a huge hit, it was more work and responsibility than Sarah wanted. The last few months she had been more focused on personal life, including her boyfriend Jared Greene's exhibit at a gallery in Prague. Sarah flew there with him for the opening while Emily housesat and Whiskey-sat, and ran the Coiffure singlehandedly. And she did a fabulous job.

"Come on, Whisk," Emily said, leading the dog to a grooming table. He needed a good brushing and a blow dry so that he'd be ready for his costume.

"I can't believe he'll wear a hat for you," Em said as she ran the brush along his spine.

He looked at her and moved his black lips into a grin.

"Well, the collared tweed cape looks dumb without it," Sarah said, picking up a brush and starting on Whiskey's right side.

"But he hates hats," Em insisted. "And besides, calling you

Sarahlock Holmes is starting to catch on around town. So shouldn't Whiskey be dressed as Watson instead of Sherlock?"

"Maybe. But I'm not really sure what Watson wore." Sarah glanced out their front window. They were half a block from Main Street, and the whole area was humming with activity. The Halloween Pet Parade had become a beloved tradition in their town, drawing families, tourists, and every canine and human companion with a festive bone in their bodies.

By mid-morning, the sidewalks were lined with hay bales and pumpkins. Black and orange streamers fluttered from the lampposts, and Cottageville Park, the endpoint of the parade, was filled with booths selling apple cider, pumpkin bars, and homemade dog treats shaped like ghosts and jack-o-lanterns. Java and Juice, which was owned by Sarah's BFF Ginger Jones and where Sarah's boyfriend worked part-time as a barista, always had the most popular booth. People stood in line a dozen deep to purchase the caramel apple scones, candied ginger rolls, and cinnamon apple tarts. The cafe had closed early to open their makeshift store at the park.

Sarah had put a table next to the Java and Juice booth, though she and Em wouldn't staff it until after the parade. They were offering free pawdicures and candy cane printed bandanas, and in the early morning, they had put up signage and organized treat samples, with obsessive precision.

And now that Whiskey was slightly damp but perfectly fluffed, Sarah attached his Sherlock collared cape and attached the hat to the top of his head with the chin strap. He promptly batted the hat with his paw and pulled it off.

"Whiskey," she said. "I thought we had a deal."

He flashed her a black lipped smile and walked to the Coiffure door, leaving the hat on the floor where it fell.

Emily chuckled. "I didn't think he'd wear it for long." She picked it up and moved the towels they had used to the washing machine and threw them in. "Come on, Sarah. I don't want to be late."

Sarah removed the denim dog print apron she was wearing and hung it on a hook. "Hang on a sec," she said, disappearing into the bathroom.

When she emerged, Emily gasped. Her eyes were wide. "No, Sarah. Seriously?" Her grin was bigger than a quokka's.

Sarah was thrilled by Em's reaction to her surprise. Sarah had donned a tweed jacket and hat that matched Whiskey. She wore a white button down shirt and tweed vest over brown pants and oxfords and she carried a magnifying glass in her hand and had an unlit pipe in her mouth.

"Stand near Whiskey. I need a photo,' Emily insisted. "This is awesome."

Sarah hammed it up in a variety of poses, hugging her dog, standing above him with her mouth agape and her index fingers and thumbs pointed like weapons down at him, inspecting him with the magnifying glass, and holding the glass up to one of his eyes.

Emily's chuckles filled the Coiffure as she captured every pose.

"Okay, okay," Sarah said. "We've gotta get going." She locked up her business and doublechecked that Em carried the box with the samples of oatmeal dog shampoo and other treats that they would hand out at their table. They walked up Main Street and headed to the park to finish their set up and to talk to clients new and old and to meet curious out-of-town pet owners. Whiskey was off-leash as usual and led the way like a parade marshal.

Jared was working the Java and Juice booth with Ginger. At one point, while he was serving a customer a cup of cider, he caught Sarah's eye and smiled. She loved his auburn-headed handsomeness, how his green eyes sparkled whenever he looked her way. Sarah's heart did a somersault. They had been a couple for almost a year, but his smiles felt as exciting as the first one he had ever given her many years ago.

The air in the park was filled with barks, laughter, children in capes and fairy wings darting between the stalls and around in circles. An occasional squeaky toy cut through the din, and the scent of baked apples, caramel, and cinnamon mixed with the woodsy notes of fallen leaves. It was the kind of the day that made Sarah feel grounded and whole. Her life in Cottageville hadn't been perfect—and some moments had been downright scary—but events like today's made her grateful for the slower pace and strong community that surrounded her, so much different than in the West Coast city where she grew up.

At three twenty-five, Mayor Trish McGowan, who was back from taking a couple-month sabbatical to attend to some personal things, kicked off the parade over a sound system with a "Happy Halloween, everyone. If you can make your way to the parade start line, we will begin shortly." Sarah and Whiskey raced through a shortcut they knew to get to the south end of Main Street. They hung back so that they were almost at the end of the participants.

Dogs of all shapes and sizes marched with their owners. Princess pugs, pirate retrievers, and one particularly proud schnauzer in a hot dog bun flaunted their stuff and stopped for photos or an occasional treat. Whiskey walked off-leash beside Sarah, trotting like he knew how good he looked...even with the hat he hated. Spectators laughed and pointed at them and some of the locals cheered at their costumes. Children waved from the sidewalks and Sarah waved in return.

They passed the town library, decorated at its entrance with dangling paper bats. Sarah waved to Carole Binds, the head librarian, who was handing out bookmarks and candy to anyone with only two legs under four feet tall.

Then, as they reached the entrance to the park near a big scarecrow display, Whiskey stopped in his tracks. His ears were rigid. He sniffed the air.

"What is it, boy?" Sarah asked, tugging gently on his collar. There weren't many people behind them, but Sarah didn't want them holding up the parade.

But Whiskey wouldn't budge. HIs whole body was stiff.

Then he barked—sharp and low—and bolted forward, dragging Sarah who still had a hold of his collar, toward the corn stalks and bales of hay that surrounded the biggest scarecrow in the center of the display.

Sarah stumbled, catching her balance just as Whiskey stopped in front of the scarecrow's feet.

"Whiskey, stop. You're going to—"

But the words died in her throat.

Whiskey had his paws on something that wasn't straw. Something pale and motionless, half-hidden behind a pumpkin.

Sarah blinked.

But the thing didn't change or move.

It was a hand.

A real, human hand.

Her stomach lurched.

She pulled her phone from her pocket and called Police Chief James Order. After all of the mysteries she had stumbled across in the last two years, she had him on speed dial. "Come quickly to the park entrance," she said, "to the big scarecrow display. Whiskey found someone and they aren't moving."

She disconnected and moved closer. Sarah pushed aside the corn husks and hay. What she uncovered made her gasp.

There, beneath the big scarecrow lay a man dressed in a costume nearly identical to the big scarecrow. He wore a brown jacket, a plaid shirt, and had straw stuffed in his sleeves. Only he wasn't part of the official display. He was human. And he was dead.

Sarah swallowed hard and looked at the man's face. His head was lolled to the side at an unnatural angle. His skin was pale, his lips tinged blue. And though Sarah didn't know him well, she recognized him. Paul Whitmore.

He was new to Cottageville and kept to himself. He had moved into Micas Brighton's house after Micas's death when his daughter Lottie—who lived in Los Angeles—decided to keep the house and rent it out.

Whiskey sat beside Paul's body, calm but alert, as if he was guarding the scene.

Sarah knelt beside her dog and put her fingers against Paul's wrist, seeing if he was warm or cold.

She didn't realize the parade had stopped behind her and that a crowd was now forming, until she heard Chief James' voice of authority yell, "Coming through. Step aside, people. Let the police through."

Sarah didn't move. Her heart was pounding. Questions flooded her brain: *Why had Paul moved here? Why was he dressed like a scarecrow? He didn't have a pet in the parade. Who would want him dead?*

She looked up at the scarecrow looming above them. It had a pumpkin head with a crooked painted grin.

But that grin no longer looked cheerful.

Chief James greeted Sarah and checked the body. HIs officers had people step back and they put up yellow tape. They secured the perimeter and began taking statements of those in the crowd.

Sarah talked to Officer John Beams and gave her official statement.

Jared came for Sarah and thrust a cup of warm cider into her hands. "You're in shock, sweetie. Drink it." He scratched Whiskey's head. "Good boy. Such a good boy."

Sarah took a sip of the cider. It tasted like cinnamon, apple, and confusion. Her eyes met Jared's. "I can't believe he's dead."

Jared put his arms around her. "I didn't know him well. People said he was quiet, didn't bother anyone."

Sarah frowned. "But someone bothered him. Maybe even enough to dress him like a scarecrow and leave him there. That's not random. That's a message." She shivered.

Emily approached them, her arms wrapped around her chest like she was trying to comfort herself. "Sarah. It's so creepy. Like a

Halloween horror movie. But real." She looked like she might vomit.

"We're going to find out who did this," Sarah whispered to Emily and Jared. She stroked Whiskey's fur with the fingers of her right hand.

Jared sighed. "Sarah, maybe we should let the police handle this one."

But Sarah was already thinking about Paul Whitmore's quiet demeanor. About how Carole Binds had helped him look through the library's archives. Carole said he asked odd questions about the town's history. He had asked her and others about an old photograph he was trying to find.

Sarah's mind spun as leaves skittered across the path at her feet.

Whiskey's ear twitched.

The parade was over.

But something else had just begun. And that started with Sarah's promise to a dead man she barely knew: *I will find your killer. And not just because Whiskey and I are dressed like Sherlock Holmes. But because everyone deserves justice.*

Sign up to follow Faith Walker and to never miss another Whiskey Dog Mystery release. Go to http://www.whiskeydogmysteries.com or follow us on social media @whiskeydogmysteries.